D0467109

# INCH BY INCH

By Morgan Llywelyn from Tom Doherty Associates

*After Rome*
*Bard: The Odyssey of the Irish*
*Brendán*
*Brian Boru*
*Drop by Drop*
*The Elementals*
*Etruscans* (with Michael Scott)
*Finn Mac Cool*
*Grania*
*The Horse Goddess*
*Inch by Inch*
*The Last Prince of Ireland*
*Lion of Ireland*
*Only the Stones Survive*
*Pride of Lions*
*Strongbow*
*The Wind from Hastings*

THE NOVELS OF THE IRISH CENTURY

*1916: A Novel of the Irish Rebellion*
*1921: A Novel of the Irish Civil War*
*1949: A Novel of the Irish Free State*
*1972: A Novel of Ireland's Unfinished Revolution*
*1999: A Novel of the Celtic Tiger and the Search for Peace*

MORGAN LLYWELYN

# INCH BY INCH

**TOR**

A TOM DOHERTY ASSOCIATES BOOK

NEW YORK

INCH BY INCH

Copyright © 2019 by Morgan Llywelyn

A Tor Book
Published by Tom Doherty Associates
120 Broadway
New York, NY 10271

www.tor-forge.com

Tor® is a registered trademark of Macmillan Publishing Group, LLC.

The Library of Congress Cataloging-in-Publication Data is available upon request.

ISBN 978-0-7653-8869-8 (hardcover)
ISBN 978-0-7653-8871-1 (ebook)

Our books may be purchased in bulk for promotional, educational, or business use. Please contact your local bookseller or the Macmillan Corporate and Premium Sales Department at 1-800-221-7945, extension 5442, or by email at MacmillanSpecialMarkets@macmillan.com.

First Edition: August 2019

Printed in the United States of America

0 9 8 7 6 5 4 3 2 1

*For Richard Lovelock, whose theory inspired this story,*
*Richard Johnson, who made quantum physics a challenge,*
*and Brian Cox, who knows the answers are found in the cosmos*

# INCH BY INCH

# 1

The patrons of Bill's Bar and Grill stared in astonishment at the stocky figure of Morris Saddlethwaite. He stood in the front doorway waving one arm; his normally florid face was ashen. The sleeve of his jacket was thickly smeared with something resembling dried blood. "I don't think you can move your car, Jack," he said to a man sitting at the nearest table. "I just brushed against your fender and this stuff came off on my clothes." The arm-waving became frenetic. "The goddamned metal's rotting!"

Jack Reece raised a sardonic eyebrow. "What's this, Morris? Some joke you found in the bottom of a bottle?"

"It's not a joke and I'm not drunk, I wish I was. A couple minutes ago this grunge on my arm was part of your fuckin' fender. If you didn't make a habit of parking that old heap so it blocks the sidewalk—"

"That old heap," Jack interrupted, "is a vintage Ford Mustang convertible, a certified classic car that's worth more than your whole miserable carcass." His pale gray eyes were like shards of ice. "If you've damaged it in any way—"

"It's damaged me, more like. How'm I s'posed to get this shit off?"

Seated across the table from Jack, Shay Mulligan brushed a lock of coppery hair away from his eyes and leaned forward for a look. "It doesn't look like shit to me," he said, "and it appears to be falling off on its own."

"Onto my clean floor," Bill Burdick complained as he tossed a towel over his shoulder and stepped out from behind the bar. "Stop waving that mess around, Morris; you're gonna have to mop it up. Why'd you bring it in here, anyway?"

"What else could I do? Have a little sympathy, will ya?"

"Sympathy for what?" asked Gerry Delmonico. "Is that stuff burning your arm?"

Saddlethwaite looked at the arm in question. "Well, no. I mean not yet, not exactly, but—"

"Then what happened?"

"You tell me," the afflicted man said piteously. He lowered his arm but held it as far away from the rest of his body as possible, as if the limb were a snake that might bite him.

Tables, booths and barstools were evacuated in the rush to examine the novelty and offer opinions. A babble of voices vied for supremacy. One phrase above others was frequently repeated.

The Change.

Jack Reece stayed in his seat and said nothing. During the recent crisis his steadiness had given his friends courage. When others experienced a temporary loss of sanity as profound as if they had seen the law of gravity repealed, Jack had been scared too.

But he never let it show.

Orphaned young, he had been raised by his mother's unmarried sister. Beatrice Fontaine was devoted to the boy. She was intensely self-reliant and had encouraged the same quality in her nephew, together with a determination to keep personal matters private. These strengthened his natural tendency to be a lone wolf. They also gave him an air of mystery that others found irresistible. Many women—and not a few men—gazed at him with a speculative expression in their eyes. He had learned to recognize the signs early on, and to discourage them, if he chose, without any hurt feelings.

In this way Jack Reece had reached the dawn of his fourth decade as a confirmed bachelor. Then came the Change. The unexpected, inexplicable and worldwide disintegration of most plastic.

Still watching Saddlethwaite, Jack automatically reached to give a comforting pat to the shoulder that should have been next to his.

She wasn't there.

Only Lila Ragland, sitting beside Shay Mulligan, noted Jack's hastily aborted gesture. In the list of names she carried in her brain a checkmark was erased from one column and added to another.

The third time he heard someone say "change," Jack Reece

pushed back his chair and stood up. Without raising his voice he could command attention. Tall and sinewy, with a hawkish nose and thick black hair starting to go silver at the temples, he looked like a man who could handle himself in a fight—which was why he rarely had to fight.

"Hold on, everybody," he said, "there's bound to be a simple explanation for this, and it isn't the Change."

"Didn't a drunk run into your car a while back?" Burdick asked. "Did a lot of damage? As I recall it was in the garage for weeks. What if—"

"That was a long time ago, Bill, and if you're suggesting that Bud Moriarty used plastic anywhere in my car you're dead wrong. He wouldn't dare. Even the paint's polymer-free, just like the original. She may be an antique, but she's as authentic as the day she came out of the factory."

"Yeah, but just suppose—"

Jack was exasperated. In spite of the effort the town was making to return to normalcy, many people were still nervous, as easily stampeded as cattle spooked by lightning. "What's happened to my car has nothing to do with the Change," he said flatly. "That's definitely over." He looked to the woman on the other side of the table. "You're the journalist, Lila, you tell them."

She nodded her agreement. "It's over, all right, the international media confirmed it last year. The final event was reported from North Korea, so you wouldn't call it trustworthy, but the Change has been relegated to the history books. Your car must have been damaged by something else . . . and I'm sorry about it," she added with a smile he couldn't help returning.

Most men smiled at Lila Ragland. Her high cheekbones and tilted green eyes added a touch of the exotic to the prosaic Midwestern town of Sycamore River.

Jack Reece never acted on the flicker of lust she caused in him, but he would not deny it either.

Morris Saddlethwaite appropriated what remained of Shay's beer, wiped his mouth on his uncontaminated sleeve and plonked the glass back on the table. "You better come outside and see for yourself, Jack."

Jack followed him outside, trailed by the other patrons of the bar and grill. Even Marla, who was Bill's divorced sister-in-law, abandoned the kitchen where she created bar food of exceptional quality in a space not much larger than a king-sized bed. Given her size it was surprising she could fit in, but as any man who danced with her could testify, she was amazingly light on her feet. Marla's hair this week was dyed an improbable shade of plum and swirled into a fake chignon.

When she saw Jack's car she let out a squeak like a mouse.

In the soft light of an overcast afternoon Jack's scarlet Mustang straddled the curb close to the front door. This was his customary parking place. Everyone who entered Bill's noticed the car.

Today everyone noticed the distorted metal that sagged

from the driver's side of the convertible like frosting from a warm cake.

Nestled in the lush valley of a winding river and surrounded by rolling farmland, Sycamore River was a large small town, or a small large town, depending upon the point of view. It was a peaceful place, devoid of traffic noise. Automobiles had become scarce. Trucks were even more rare, and there were no motorized buses.

For over three decades of the twenty-first century the roads in and out of town and along the urban streets had hummed with traffic. Modern vehicles had employed a wide variety of materials in their manufacture, including countless items disguised as something else, a fact that was shockingly demonstrated during the worldwide disintegration of plastic.

Hardly anything was what it had appeared to be. Wood, metal, stone, pottery, fabric; everything from a child's toboggan to the fittings in the space shuttle. Imposters.

The phenomenon known as the Change had forced a return to earlier technologies. Industries of every kind were frantically retooling. Almost nothing had been lost that could not be replaced—except a number of innocent lives and a lot of faith in the material era—but rebuilding required a leap of imagination.

Preplastic cars like the vintage convertible had acquired iconic status overnight.

The crowd gathered around Jack's red Mustang were visibly shocked at its desecration.

His control deserted him. "Who the hell blowtorched my car!"

Edgar Tilbury stepped forward to run a gnarled forefinger down what had been a door. The slumping metal felt grainy. So did the oddly folded fender. Neither was soft, yet they were not quite hard. Glancing over his shoulder, Tilbury asked in a voice like a rusty hinge, "When did you park here, Jack?"

"Less than ten minutes ago. You saw Gerry and me come in; we sat down at the front table with Shay and Lila."

Tilbury straightened up. "Was the car like this then?"

"I sure as hell would have noticed! How about you, Gerry?"

Gerry Delmonico was a lanky man with an easy smile and skin the color of dark chocolate. He was not smiling now, but staring at the car in disbelief. "It was fine when we left your aunt's house, I'd swear to it."

"This wasn't a torch job," Tilbury stated flatly. "The metal's as cold as an auditor for the IRS. You got another 'simple' explanation, Jack?"

"How about acid?" Evan Mulligan wondered. "Could someone have, like, thrown acid on the car?" At nineteen he was a strikingly handsome young man, with his father's reddish-gold hair and the finely chiseled features of his long-dead mother, but the turmoil of the Change had corresponded with his passage through puberty. Behind his good looks was a moody and complicated spirit.

"That's a good guess, Evan," said Gerry, "but no acid could have worked that fast and left the metal cold by the time we came out."

"Are you sure?"

"I was an industrial chemist before your father and I started the River Valley Transportation Service," Gerry reminded Evan. "Now I drive a carriage for a living, and intriguing as this is, I have to get the horses ready for the afternoon circuit. Can't leave paying customers waiting when it looks like it's going to start raining again."

"I better get moving too," said Shay Mulligan. "My waiting room's going to be full after lunch. Dogs and cats and maybe a python with a bellyache."

Jack was eyeing the damaged Mustang with the expression of a man afraid he would have to put his dog to sleep. "My car's not going to move until my mechanic takes a look at it. Trying to drive it could do irreparable damage."

"You can't leave it here blocking my door!"

"Fair enough, Bill. If several of you lend a hand, maybe we can inch it out of the way."

The process was slow, the volunteers nervous. They treated the car as if it were packed with dynamite. In spite of their care a little more material fell off and lay like a puddle of drying blood on the pavement.

When the entrance to the bar was clear Jack turned to Gerry Delmonico. "If you're driving to the north side will you pick up Bud Moriarty for me? His garage is right on your route; I'll phone to let him know what's happened and you can bring him back here." As he spoke Jack used thumb and forefinger to retrieve an object from the inside pocket of his jacket. In its worn fabric cover, the device might have been a case for sunglasses instead of an all-purpose communicator relying on satellite transmission.

Bill's sister-in-law eyed it with curiosity. "Is that an All-Com? It looks different."

He held it up to show her. "I've carried it for years; it's one of the lightweight aluminum models the Japanese made to replace environmentally unfriendly smartphones. Our government was on a 'Buy American' kick so the idea was never promoted over here, which is too bad. Mine's powered by small hydrogen cells, I just vent the water vapor. All-Coms are like sports cars, Marla; the older the better."

"That's what I keep telling the ladies," Tilbury quipped while Jack instructed his all-purpose communicator. By the time Bud's face appeared on the three-dimensional screen he was already talking; the device recorded his words from the beginning.

Their conversation was terse. Bud Moriarty seemed to think Jack had wrecked the car but wouldn't admit it. He made explanatory gestures in the air while the mechanic watched from the screen. "I don't know what you're talking about, Jack. That doesn't make any sense. The climate may have gone to hell but cars don't melt in the rain."

"It hasn't melted, that's what I keep trying to tell you. If anything, it's collapsed."

"What are you drinking over there? Bill serves good booze, but I've never seen you in the bag this early in the day."

"I'm perfectly sober, Bud. You can judge the condition of my car for yourself."

"I'm afraid I can't take time to come to the south side today; I'm waiting for a tool delivery and it's overdue already."

"Then I'll bring my car to you. I can't leave it like this."

The mechanic laughed. "Maybe you should sober up first, pal."

When the AllCom clicked off Jack asked Evan Mulligan to run an errand for him. He slipped the boy some money and gave him a slap on the shoulder. "Quick as you can," he stressed. "We have to take the Mustang across the river."

Lila said, "I'd love to hear what your mechanic says about your car, but I'm afraid *The Sycamore Seed* doesn't approve of its reporters taking long lunches unless there's a story in it. Vandalism doesn't rate much of a headline."

"You'll have a headline murder if I catch the bastard who's responsible," Jack replied grimly.

"Come on, Lila," said Shay. "I'll walk you as far as the newspaper office. From there I can jog to my clinic in fifteen minutes."

The Change had taught people to measure a distance by how long it took on foot.

As the pair began to walk Lila linked his arm with hers. She pressed it tightly against her side. Body to body; heat to heat. Shay felt the familiar thickening in his throat. To distract himself from the sensation he asked, "Do you really think Jack's car was vandalized? Sycamore River's a law-abiding town."

"It used to be," she corrected. "Don't forget that during the Change mental disorders multiplied all over the world. Gloria Delmonico's a psychologist; she explained to me that living under unnatural stress could bend human beings all out of shape. We aren't emotionally able to cope with the incomprehensible. Remember the articles I wrote about the epidemic of random violence? People you'd never expect were suddenly snapping and attacking whoever was nearest. The killings on the day of Jack's wedding were one example; vandalism may be another symptom."

"I'd call throwing acid on a valuable car more than a symptom, Lila. No way it was done on the spur of the moment; who carries around a bottle of acid in his pocket?"

"You heard what Gerry said, it wasn't acid. And are you sure it was a man who did it? Enemies come in all sizes and sexes, and Jack's left a trail of broken hearts behind him if the rumors are true."

"But who would know how to cause damage like that? Wait a minute . . ." Shay snapped his fingers. "Jack used to do some work for Robert Bennett, didn't he? There were plenty of rumors about the things Bennett manufactured out there at his factory in the woods. Crates were shipped out every week by overseas carriers. Parts for munitions, that's what the police determined later from the stuff they found in the wreckage. Probably to be sold abroad; preparing for war is the biggest business on the planet. Bennett was a nasty piece of work; his own dog didn't like him, Lila."

"Neither did Gerry Delmonico, even though he worked for him. You can say one thing about Bennett; he seems to have paid well. But he died in the explosion at his factory." Lila stopped walking and turned to Shay with a question in her eyes. "And now Jack's engaged to his widow. Do you think that—"

"No, I don't. Jack didn't start going out with Nell Bennett until months after her husband was buried. Even a bastard like Robert Bennett couldn't rise from the dead to attack his wife's new lover. You reporters are always looking for a story."

"I don't make them up."

"I didn't say you did."

"But you have to admit, given the coincidences, that—"

"I don't have to admit anything, Lila; Jack's a good friend of mine. He has his faults, but I'd be willing to bet money he never made a pass at a married woman. It just wouldn't be his style. Besides, I thought you liked him."

"I do, very much, but he's so damned sure about everything. How can he be so confident all the time? Someday Jack Reece is going to run into something he can't cope with; something harder to deal with than the Change. I only hope I'm around to see it."

# 2

---

Bill's Bar and Grill was the unofficial meeting place of the Wednesday Club: men and women of varying ages and backgrounds but with one thing in common: passionately devoted to discussion and debate, they were the linear heirs of the men who used to lounge on the courthouse steps.

The atmosphere was perfect for them. Pine paneling and scuffed oak floors, a well-stocked bar where regulars could keep their own bottles, framed hunting prints on the walls, and a kitchen that could be relied upon for anything from early breakfasts to late suppers. The wooden barstools were thickly padded with folded blankets. There was fabric upholstery instead of imitation leather seating in the booths. Light was supplied by scores of strategically placed beeswax candles.

Closing time was determined by the intensity of the conversation.

Following the Change nothing in Bill's could be described as "modern," except the hospitality.

After Evan Mulligan left on his errand, Jack Reece went inside and ordered a beer. "You oughta have some lunch while you wait," Bill advised him. "I can recommend the chicken fried steak, it's on special today."

"Marla," Jack called to the unseen presence who had now returned to the kitchen, "you still putting cumin and horseradish in the batter?"

"Don't go telling my secrets," she called back.

"If I wasn't engaged I'd ask you to marry me."

Marla peered around the kitchen door. "I'm too good for you, Jack Reece. If only I had a waist I'd have an hourglass figure."

While Bill accompanied Morris Saddlethwaite to the men's room to clean up, Edgar Tilbury eased into the seat Shay had vacated. Tilbury was grizzled and lean, an ageless man. Time was gnawing the flesh from his bones, but beneath eyebrows like a bank of briars his eyes remained preternaturally bright. After selling the large engineering firm he had founded, Tilbury claimed to be retired. No one believed him. He could not sit still for five minutes. "That man has no off switch," Bea Fontaine had once remarked.

"I agree with you, Jack," he said now. "The damage to your car had nothing to do with the Change. God knows we saw enough of that to recognize it. No matter what Gerry Delmonico thinks, someone used acid on your car. Or hit it with—"

"With what? A battering ram? And how come we didn't hear anything when we were sitting in here only a few yards away?"

"I don't know, but tell me when you find out, will you? I can guarantee it won't be a weird phenomenon like the Change. Speaking of which, I think we dodged a bullet there."

"How do you figure that, Edgar? The whole civilized world suffered from the Change. We learned the hard way that much of what we thought was 'real' was made from petrochemicals."

"Plastic," Edgar said, as if the word left a bad taste in his mouth.

"Yeah. The so-called miracle material." Jack adopted what his Aunt Bea called his "lecturing voice"; one familiar to the members of the Wednesday Club, where he loved to hold forth. "Earlier in this century the steel industry in the West was nearly destroyed by Chinese and Russian competition. If that wasn't bad enough, low-cost foreign imports of consumer goods were bankrupting American retailers. But we found a way to compete. Good old plastic. Cheap to manufacture, endlessly malleable, light to ship and easy to store. Almost anything could be replicated and sold for more than it was worth. As long as it looked real that was what mattered to the man in the street—until the damned stuff started dissolving for no known reason and we had a total disaster on our hands."

"You can't call it total," said Tilbury. He tugged at his left earlobe, a lifelong habit that had left that portion of his anatomy unnaturally long. His deeply lined face resembled that of an evil gnome. "Remember how things were before the Change? Interconnectivity was the buzzword; your phone talked to your house, which talked to your car, which talked to your bank, which could be accessed by any practiced hacker with a computer the size of a playing card.

"Technology wasn't a bad thing, Jack. Like fire and electricity, it was neutral, neither good nor evil. But we could shape it for our own purposes. And did we ever!

"Back in 2020 it was estimated that the internet of *things* connected to other *things* included billions of items in the US alone. There were no secrets and no privacy. Cyber had become a military platform like land and sea and air. From cyberspace a hostile force could cripple the Pentagon without losing a soldier. Try as they might, our Cyber Command and Europol's Cyber Crime Headquarters couldn't cope.

"That was only the tip of the iceberg. Terrorist activities were organized through the virtual world; no part of the globe was immune. Malware attacks disrupted governments and crippled institutions. There was so much 'fake news' no one knew who or what to believe anymore. Pedophiles had an unlimited hunting ground. Internet trolls bullied kids and adults into suicide; election campaigns were hacked and rigged; and who-knew-what giant spiders were pulling the strings of the Web, instigating proxy wars for their own benefit."

Jack raised a protesting hand. "Stop it, Edgar; you're depressing me more than I already was."

When Tilbury chuckled his features rearranged themselves from evil gnome to cheerful dwarf. "Then let's look at the good news. Intelligence technology employed countless plastic components, large and small, that were affected by the Change. When most of them collapsed the tyranny of the internet went with them. The techies screamed blue murder and country after country accused its enemies of industrial sabotage, but in the long run it was a blessing. We didn't know what caused the Change and we couldn't stop it, but voilà! A huge problem had been solved. *That's* what I mean by saying we dodged a bullet."

"I can't agree with you," Jack said. "I'm one of those techies you mentioned; I used the internet extensively to do business and for a lot of my daily life. The net changed the world more than anything in the history of man. Giving up its advantages is like giving up fire. Should we start over from scratch, pre-Alan Turing? Besides, the Change wasn't a natural phenomenon like an earthquake. I'm convinced some human agency was behind it, which would mean the problem may not be solved after all, just redirected."

Tilbury snorted. "Who says it wasn't natural? There's a lot of weird natural phenomena you wouldn't believe if you didn't see it with your own eyes. You ever hear of snow being rolled into cylinders by the wind? It happens in parts of the UK. And water runs uphill in a place in Arkansas. Hell, nobody even heard of dinosaurs until some fellow called Buckland found the jawbone of a Megalosaurus in Oxfordshire. After that people started discovering fossils all over the place. They were fairly popping out of the dirt in the American Southwest.

"I tell you, Jack, this old planet's undergone a lot of changes in several billion years. The question is, What next? The internet's gone and so are its demon offspring like the Dark Web. Good riddance, I say. War's still with us, of course; mankind's not ready to give up anything that profitable. National economies and foreign dictators depend on it, that's why diplomacy ultimately fails.

"The future's a blank page, Jack. There was no such thing as plastic until the last century and we got along fine without it. We will again, maybe better than ever. A small amount survived for some inexplicable reason when the Change stopped abruptly, but manufacturers were already making replacements out of other materials. The possibilities are almost endless, and not as destructive to the environment as plastic was."

"You really have a down on plastic, don't you?"

"All I'm saying is we don't *need* it. Every time you drank coffee out of a plastic cup degraded petrocarbons wound up in your bloodstream. Hello, cancer. Pristine beaches were ruined by tons of plastic rubbish that washed ashore, and worst of all, whales by the thousands were dying with plastic in their bellies. We paid a terrible price for 'cheap and convenient.'"

"Lila told me you're a survivalist, Edgar, but there must be some exceptions to your creed. You live out in the country, you can't go to the corner supermarket every ten minutes. What do you store your perishables in?"

"Glass bottles and jars; I have a huge supply. And that's not all I have; you should take a look at what I've done since I sold my engineering firm. There are other ways to live a good life without making the planet uninhabitable."

In the presence of a fanatic—and Jack had long since determined that Edgar Tilbury was a fanatic, if a well-meaning one—he never argued. "Nell Bennett would be inclined to agree," he said politely.

"Where is the elegant Nell? I thought she'd be with you."

"We're not exactly together right now, Edgar."

"You two have a fight?"

"Nothing like that. But having three men die violent deaths almost in her face on our wedding day—nobody thought Dwayne Nyeberger would hide in the shrubbery outside the chapel and murder Hooper Watson, or that he and Sheriff Whittaker would kill each other in a shoot-out—well, how could Nell cope with that? As you know, we postponed the wedding. Now she's drawn into herself. Doesn't want to see anybody, just stays at home with her kids."

"Natural reaction. She's been through a lot; she'll get over it."

"I'm not sure, Edgar. Nell's pretty sensitive."

"She's pretty, period, but I suspect she's tougher than she looks; women who come from old money tend to have steel spines."

Jack could feel his emotional shields going up. "Maybe. But if things don't work out for us . . . *c'est la vie,* as my Aunt Bea says."

The older man's eyes twinkled. "Now your Aunt Bea—she's my type. Smart as paint and a healthy armful of woman. It was a waste for her to be working in the bank."

"Old Man Staunton would rather have cut his throat than let her go. She practically ran the S and S Mercantile before it went out of business."

At that moment Bill Burdick set a heaping platter in front of Jack. "Enjoy, but I warn you. If that doesn't come back empty Marla'll march out here and knock your block off. She's not only built like a tank; she has a mean left hook."

Jack pushed the platter toward Tilbury. "Share this with me?"

"Don't like fried steak," he stated while forking the largest piece from the platter onto a side plate and topping it with a generous handful of French fries. As a crowning touch he emptied a paper cup of blue cheese dressing over the concoction.

Jack raised an eyebrow. "You sure that's enough for you?"

"I can come back for more if I need to." Tilbury cut off a large bite of steak, put it in his mouth and rolled his eyes in appreciation. "Damn, that's good," he said around a mouthful of masticated meat. "Y'know, it's hard for me to imagine Lila as a banker's granddaughter. Good thing she inherited his brains instead of his looks. I was in school with Oliver Staunton, guess that's why I've always felt paternal toward her; that and the fact that my late wife and I couldn't have children. I took Lila under my wing when she came back to town. She even lived out at my place for a while, but she's too much of a city girl to be happy in the country. Claimed the crickets kept her awake."

"I don't know any woman less in need of a father figure than Lila Ragland."

"And I thought you had a reputation as a ladies' man," Tilbury teased. "You don't know the first thing about them."

"I'm beginning to suspect you're right," Jack agreed.

"Is your mechanic coming over here?"

"No, I'm going to try to take Mustang to him. It's like seeing an animal in pain, I'm anxious to put her out of her misery."

The skin around Tilbury's eyes pleated with amusement. "Only Americans anthropomorphize their cars."

"I'm not sure that's true. Besides, when you live with something as long as I've lived with that car, it's impossible not to."

"You'd better face the fact that it has a limited life span, then. So does everything we love," Tilbury added. He sat motionless for a moment, lost in thought. Then said briskly, "How're you going to transport it?"

"Evan's gone to borrow a team and a flatbed hay trailer to carry the car across the river; he should be back soon. It's a good thing Sycamore River's turned more agricultural since the Change."

"Mind if I ride over with you? I'd like to see this."

By the time everything was ready the cloudy afternoon was fading toward a darker evening. The rain had not begun to fall but the smell of it was in the air. After much effort, most of it devoted to keeping the body from falling apart, Jack's damaged car was on the trailer and buttressed by bales of hay. He and Edgar seated themselves next to it, dangling their feet over the edge of the flatbed. Evan Mulligan took the driver's seat, expertly handling the reins of a pair of shaggy-legged farm horses.

"You can't beat *real* horsepower," he called over his shoulder as he clucked to the team.

Jack laughed. "That boy's an anachronism."

"Not an anachronism," Tilbury countered, "he's just a kid who loves horses. His father's a veterinarian now, but Shay rode a lot when he was a boy, even did some show jumping. So it must be in Evan's genes. The horse-and-buggy era suits him right down to the ground; maybe he's ahead of his time and not behind it."

"Some of us are like that. Me, for instance. When I bought

my farm it had just what I was looking for: plenty of distance from the neighbors, fertile soil for growing vegetables and a good artesian well. Plus I'd have the space to indulge a new hobby after I retired—building and selling model carriages. I thought I could make a profit re-creating the elegance of an unhurried era. But you know Murphy's Law? 'Whatever can go wrong, will.' I'd overlooked the fact that most folks want everything brand-new; they prefer to spend their money on cars that cost a fortune to run and lose all their value in a few years."

"The automobile's hard to kill, Edgar. Machines all over the world are being redesigned now. In a few years my car will probably be in a museum." Jack turned to look at the Mustang, crouched behind them like an injured baby dinosaur.

The image made him wince.

He shifted his gaze to the scene around him. A picture of suburban serenity—aside from the growl of a power mower. Tree-lined streets and houses surrounded with landscaped shrubbery; tempting smells wafting from the open windows of kitchens where meals were actually cooking, rather than being microwaved. Many of the houses had double garages that had been converted into two box stalls for horses, or one stall plus space for an automobile shrouded in tarpaulin. The cost of riding lessons had been added to household budgets.

The scene might almost have come from a Norman Rockwell painting. It was hard to remember what it had looked like . . . before.

The team pulling the trailer exchanged whinnied greetings with horses who were waiting for their evening oats. A woman called her family in for supper. There were other sounds too; an ancient gramophone with its distinctive voice.

*Who in the world still has one of those?*

Jack experienced a troubling sense of disassociation; something he had felt once or twice before in his life. It was like looking through someone else's eyes.

He gripped the edge of the wagon with both hands.

"This doesn't seem real," he said to Tilbury.

"Hunh?"

"You and me riding on a hay wagon in the twilight."

"Sure beats the hell out of being caught in a traffic jam on the freeway."

"I'll be glad when things get back to normal."

"You think they will? And what's 'normal' anyway?" Tilbury squinted at Jack's face. "At a guess, I'd say you don't go in for nostalgia."

"Not really; my Mustang's an exception. The future's what attracts me. I want to know what's coming next; what's around the next corner or up the next street."

"Trouble, most likely," said Tilbury. "Work and trouble and . . . what sort of work do you do, Jack? I've never heard you say, but you seem to have plenty of free time on your hands."

They were approaching the river. The smell came to meet them: the green mossy aroma of water winding between hills strung together like a row of vertebrae.

River perfume, rain in the air, night closing softly over.

"Time is one thing nobody ever has enough of," Jack said softly. It was his turn for a moment of reflection. "To answer your question, I'm a freelance agent. I locate people who have particular items to sell and bring them together with buyers. If I make a big enough sale I take a few months of my retirement in advance while I'm still young enough to enjoy it."

"That's a damned good idea," said Tilbury. "Was it part of your arrangement with Robert Bennett?"

Jack chose to deflect. "When you sold that business of yours what did you do with the money?"

"Put it in a hole in the ground."

"I was being serious, Edgar."

"So am I. When I retired my money went into a hole in the ground. Lila could tell you all about my . . . my bolt-hole. You know what that is? The last refuge of a sane human being.

"This world isn't sane, Jack. Maybe it was once, but no more. For a long time now, deranged politicians and professional hate mongers have been threatening each other with annihilation and demanding the rest of us accept their craziness as normal. I refuse. You could say I'm the ultimate rebel.

"Since I sold my engineering firm I don't even have a computer. I need to write something down I've got a pencil and a notebook. I'm not *dis*connected, I'm *un*connected from the egomaniacs who try to rule us through algorithms. I've lived long enough to watch the process develop and I'm disgusted. For humanity we've substituted digitization. Count me out. I've created a refuge for myself and a few intelligent humans so I'll have someone to talk to. If the trolls take over we won't be available."

"*Whew,*" Jack whistled. "You make a lot of sense, though I wouldn't have thought so a few years ago. Step by step, I was accepting the world you just outlined. That was the way things were, I thought. Before the Change the first thing I did every morning was check the news on my AllCom to give myself a good scare and get the adrenaline pumping. Real Doomsday stuff. Us against them, countries competing for diminishing resources, enough wars to justify the massive expenditures of the industrial-military complexes and no end in sight. I got used to it. Most of us did; it was the new normal.

"Ever since the third time the Russians staged the World Cup in Saint Petersburg we've known they could achieve anything they set out to do. With the seas rising around the world, they're making plans to colonize the rest of the solar system. They'll plant their flag on Mars and have a welcome wagon to greet us when we get there."

"I don't know about that," Tilbury said. "If we can believe the world news, the Change seems to have dampened down their aggression a bit. Too bad it hasn't affected everyone that way. I'd rather fight the Russians than the enemy we have now; we never should have meddled in Asia. But in spite of all the ranting and raving I'd like to think there'll be no war and the human race will succumb to an attack of common sense."

"You don't really believe that."

Tilbury sighed. "Not on your life, Jack, if you'll pardon the bad pun. Come take a look at my bolt-hole sometime. See what I've done. I think you'll be surprised."

"Thanks, Edgar, I might do that."

A schoolteacher on a gray mare, trotting home with a saddlebag full of papers to grade, cast a curious glance at the car perched on the trailer but only said, "Swing that rig wide before you go onto the bridge. You'll want a straight shot at it."

The team successfully negotiated the turn onto the bridge across the Sycamore River and headed up the street toward Bud's house. The asphalt paving the street had been a victim of the Change, leaving an underbed of rough gravel. Horseshoes rang music from the stones.

Lacey Strawbridge, Bud's longtime housemate, was waiting beside him on the front porch. When she saw the damaged car she gave a shriek. "Oh Jack, your beautiful *car*!!! That's absolutely the *saddest* thing I *ever saw*!"

Bud said, "Don't get so worked up, Lace, maybe I can fix it."

She punched his arm. "You always say that, you mechanic you. But what about my washer-dryer? And the burglar alarm that kept going off in the middle of the night? Your way to fix that was to rip it off the wall."

Out of the side of his mouth Edgar muttered to Jack, "That is the skinniest woman I ever saw. If she turned sideways she wouldn't cast a shadow."

"She'd be thrilled to hear you say that. Lacey's a fiend for exercise and low-calorie foods; if she gains an ounce she stops eating for a week."

They did not unload the Mustang until they reached Moriarty's Garage, a low frame building roofed with corrugated tin, two blocks from the house. Above the office door a sign advertised REPAIRS, SPARE PARTS, AND TIRES. The word TIRES was partially obscured by a line painted through it. Below was: GENUINE RUBBER TIRES AVAILABLE BY SPECIAL ORDER. THREE MONTH DELAY.

Lacey had followed on foot from the house. She watched anxiously as the men carefully maneuvered the car onto the rack and raised it over the pit. The Mustang shuddered like an animal about to be sacrificed.

"Be careful, Bud!" Lacey urged.

"No, I'm going to mess up on purpose, woman; what do you expect? This is like trying to move some damned sand castle."

When he stood below the car, shining a massive flashlight

into the undercarriage, Bud scratched his head. "How the fuck did you do this, Jack? Jump down here with me and look how the chassis is buckled. I've never seen anything like it, even after a head-on collision."

"There wasn't any collision. I backed my car out of Bea's garage, Gerry got in and we drove to Bill's, less than two miles. No traffic, we didn't see another car on the road."

Bud looked skeptical. "That's your story. I hate to say this, old pal, but what you have here is a write-off. We can salvage the seats and tires but not much else. My advice is to buy yourself another car, unless you prefer having a horse's ass in front of you."

At Bea Fontaine's house that night Jack had no appetite for dinner. "It looked like a giant had crumpled Mustang in his hands, Aunt Bea. Had to happen sometime, I guess. Ever since the first 'flying car' parasailed across the English Channel, the automobiles I loved as a kid have been headed for extinction. The combustion engine's as dead as the dodo. Today's cars are powered by electricity and made of lightweight carbon fiber; they're a different breed entirely.

"Still, I suppose I could learn to love them. Should learn to love them. I might order one of those turbocharged models, or even an amphibian, just to be on the safe side. It would take a big chunk out of my savings, but why not? What the hell else do I have to spend it on?"

The bitterness in his voice warned Bea not to mention Nell Bennett.

Bea knew what an emotional investment her nephew had made in his car. Since his late teens Jack had painstakingly collected authentic parts for the ancient Ford he had discovered in Chilton's scrap yard. The rusting wreck had cost him his secondhand bike and a tarnished silver platter he unashamedly stole from his aunt's china cabinet, but eventually he was able to take the restored Mustang to classic car shows. The gleaming scarlet convertible was a star wherever it appeared. Men wanted to be photographed behind the wheel; pretty girls liked to sit on the fenders, showing off their legs.

When the Change struck, Jack had fled to Bud Moriarty. The two men had examined the old car thoroughly, making sure there was no trace of plastic in any form.

When her nephew parked the car in her garage he covered it with a patchwork quilt that had been a family heirloom.

Bea Fontaine thought she was acquainted with all of Jack's moods, but despondency was a new one and it worried her. The old rubber tire, rotten now, he once used as a swing still hung from the oak tree in her backyard. He had called it his spaceship and pretended he was going to the moon. The yard had echoed with his merry laughter.

She wondered, Was the boy still hidden inside the man? What would it take to bring him out again? The years were flying by; she felt them in herself. The sap was drying up. Eventually Jack would petrify if someone didn't stop him.

Eleanor Bennett was not like the women her nephew usually chose, but Bea approved of his relationship with her. The Fontaines had been friends with Nell's family for generations in the closely knit society of Sycamore River. Bea could picture Jack buying a house of his own, instead of camping in hers during his sporadic returns to Sycamore River, and settling down as a family man. Having children of his own for his Aunt Bea to spoil. For them she would buy a new tire for the spaceship in the backyard . . .

"I can't do anything about your car," Bea told her nephew, "but would you like me to have a little talk with Nell?"

"I don't think it'd do any good, Aunt Bea. She might say you were interfering and she'd hate it."

"What happened on your wedding day was awful, but she will get over it."

"Will she?" Jack sounded dubious. "I'm afraid her emotional resilience may be all used up."

On the following morning they were having their second cup of coffee when the sound of an object thudding onto the front porch caught their attention. "Norman's getting later and later with that newspaper," Bea remarked. "There was a time when a boy took pride in having the early paper route. You did."

"No, I just liked being out and about when the rest of the town was still in bed. Besides, I never did need much sleep."

"You used to claim you were in training to be an astronaut and they didn't get much sleep."

"I thought I knew everything back then," he replied. "Now it seems like the more I learn the less I know."

"That's true for all of us," his aunt said. "You want another slice of toast?"

"I guess . . . no, never mind, I'm not really hungry. I'm going down to the car dealer's this morning to do a little window-shopping; maybe I'll grab a bite in town. Is there anything I can bring you?"

"A smile?" she said hopefully.

He gave her one but his heart wasn't in it.

He went out to bring the paper in, unfolding it as he came. The kitchen with its dimity-curtained windows facing east was bright and sunny for once; no sign of the stormy weather that had become so frequent. The atmosphere was fragrant with bacon and coffee. Bea's beloved cats were giving a few last licks to their breakfast bowls. The orange cat called Apollo was purring as loudly as the coffee percolator. Shay Mulligan had neutered Apollo while he was a kitten, but as a grown cat Apollo chose to disregard the inconvenience and pursued every female cat in the neighborhood.

In the garden behind the house a mockingbird sang to define his territory.

Jack stopped in the middle of the room and stared down at the paper in his hands. Raised his eyes and looked around the sunny kitchen as if he had never seen it before. "Shit," he said clearly. "Fuck it all damned to hell."

His aunt was startled. Before she could react he held up the newspaper and turned it so she could read the headline.

## MASSIVE THERMONUCLEAR DEVICE
## EXPLODED IN BALTIC SEA

# 3

Jack Reece saw the color drain from his aunt's face.

"Thermonuclear. That means it's an atom bomb."

"Not exactly, Aunt Bea. Atom bombs involve splitting an atomic nucleus to release energy; that's called fission. Hydrogen bombs are thermonuclear, like the sun. They use an incredibly high temperature to unite atomic nuclei, which forms heavier nuclei that can release much greater quantities of energy. That's fusion. And this one was apparently tested underwater."

"It wasn't ours, was it?"

"No, Aunt Bea, not if it was in the Baltic."

"But the Change grounded so many airplanes. How could anyone drop a bomb in the sea?"

Jack's eyes were as cold as an Arctic sky. "Other countries still have some aircraft, same as we do; for some reason we don't understand the Change struck rather randomly. Many of the surviving planes belong to the military, and they have timing devices for their bombs to allow the bombers to get out of range."

"Is it that easy?"

"Killing's easy, Aunt Bea. Surviving's what's hard." He

dropped the paper on the kitchen table and went into the dining room, returning with a decanter of brandy from the sideboard. He poured a generous measure into a heavy glass. "Drink this."

"It's too early, it's too—"

"Drink it all, Aunt Bea. For a minute there I thought you were going to faint."

Her spine stiffened. "I never faint!"

Bea Fontaine did not often attend the weekly meetings of the Wednesday Club, but she decided to accompany her nephew to the one on the following Wednesday. She would not admit it but she was disinclined to be alone. Gerry Delmonico was collecting the members in the carriage affectionately known as the horse-bus and delivering them to Bill's. It would be almost like a party.

When Jack and his aunt left her house she glanced up at the emerging stars; diamond dust flung across a velvet sky. No aircraft lights were competing with them. And no storm clouds either.

Nothing to fear tonight, she assured herself.

But they'll find a way.

They who? Them, the others. The not us. The bogeys under the bed and the nightmares that wake you up sweating.

She clutched Jack's arm harder than she meant to.

He glanced down at her. "You all right, Aunt Bea?"

"I'm fine, just a little cold. Are we going to pick up Nell and take her with us?"

"If she wants to come," he said. "I was going to phone her but decided it would be better to ask in person."

Bea agreed. "It can be harder to say no to someone face-to-face. Of course she might go on her own. Does she still have that little sports car her husband gave her?" She instantly regretted the question. Her nephew never responded well to mention of Robert Bennett.

"It's up on blocks," Jack replied through stiff lips. "As soon as I have another car I'll take her anywhere she needs to go."

Eleanor Bennett, known to her many friends as Nell, lived in a gated enclave west of town. The most imposing house in a community of prestigious homes, the mock-Normandy château had been built by her late husband using profits from his business, RobBenn. There had been a time when Nell loved the house, she told Jack; but she had never mentioned loving her husband.

The house was beautiful, but he knew better than most the provenance of its funding. If he wanted to hurt Nell he could have said "Your house was built with blood money," but he would never say that to her; would never allude to the fact that he too had been partially supported by the economy of war. All that had ended with the death of Robert Bennett. So had a sizeable portion of Jack's income stream. By the time he fell in love with Nell Bennett he could not afford the kind of house he wanted to give her.

As a matter of practicality Nell and her children continued to live in Robert Bennett's house. Jack silently hated it. If they were going to spend the night together he took her to a hotel.

Gerry and the others waited in the horse-bus as he approached the Bennetts' front doors: a tall pair in the French provincial style, accented by copper carriage lamps. Nell had told him she chose the lamps herself. "One of my few selections for the house that Rob didn't veto." When Jack pressed the doorbell there was no response. It was a large house, it might take time, so he waited, then tried again.

This time he was rewarded with a volley of barking; Sheila and Shamrock, the latter known as Rocky, were the Bennetts' pedigreed Irish setters. They were breathtakingly beautiful, had cost a small fortune and would have taken any burglar straight to the family safe.

There were no knockers on the doors, only a discreet doorbell button set in the right-hand doorframe. From experience Jack knew the bell was as unobtrusive as the button and could scarcely be heard beyond the living room. He pounded a door panel with his fist. "Nell! It's me. Are you there?"

The door swung open and Jessamyn Bennett looked out at him. The two setters shoved past her and proceeded to give Jack a full-body welcome.

A willowy girl with smoky blue eyes and an oval face

wreathed with light brown curls, Jess at eighteen was a younger version of her mother.

From the waiting carriage Evan Mulligan called out, "We're going to the Wednesday Club, Jess. You want to come with us?" He was already scrambling down to offer the girl his seat.

She shook her head. "Mom's got one of her sick headaches; I better stay here with her."

"Aw, come on, your brother can look after her, can't he?"

"I wouldn't trust Colin to look after a mouse in a shoe box."

Jack said, "I didn't know Nell had sick headaches."

Jess gave him an oblique glance. "There's probably a lot about my mother you don't know."

Jack wanted her children to like him; he had thought they did. The tartness in her daughter's tone was unsettling. He wanted to say, It wasn't my fault we postponed the wedding, it was Nell's idea. But he didn't.

To his relief Nell appeared in the doorway behind her daughter. "It's all right, Jess. I forgot tonight was Wednesday."

"If you want to go we're here to take you," Jack said. "Since the news about the explosion in the Baltic there'll be a lot to discuss."

She glanced past him. "Where's your car?"

"It's a long and not very funny story. Do you want to come with us?"

She only hesitated for a moment. "Wait while I put the

dogs in the kitchen. Is there enough room in the horse-bus for my kids?"

The entire membership of the Wednesday Club was gathered in Bill's Bar and Grill. "Nobody wants to be alone right now," Bea Fontaine observed aloud.

Before getting a drink and taking a seat, Jack busied himself brushing red dog hair off his clothes. He was quickly surrounded by people asking questions about his Mustang. Ordinarily such a topic would have provoked a lengthy discussion, but not on this evening. After a brief discussion the consensus was sabotage, the villain unidentified, and the conversation moved on to the explosion in the Baltic, where the villain was known and the possible outcome frightening.

"Everything is relative," said Arthur Hannisch. "Here's us thinking the Change was the worst thing that could happen, then along comes the threat of rising seas and nuclear war. Dissolving plastic doesn't seem so bad."

Bill Burdick said, "Surely to God no one can wage nuclear war without computers."

"There are a few left, remember, and you can bet the tech industry's developing replacements," Tilbury responded. "Setting off an underwater explosion in the Baltic could even be called progress by some standards. We're enjoying a little hiatus that won't last long. Watch this space."

"Damn them all!" Gloria Delmonico burst out, disturbing her infant son, who had been asleep in his carrier. "Why can't we just live in peace?"

Jack said, "Other nations are blaming us for the dramatic change in the climate, remember? We started phasing out the burning of fossil fuels a little too late; we've become the enemy now."

"They all waited too long," said Shay. "Humans are great at self-justification, though. That's what separates us from the animals."

Evan said, "I opt for the animals every time." Feeling Jessamyn Bennett's eyes on him, he gave her a surreptitious wink. "Almost every time, I mean. But I don't think we should be too scared. This planet's been under the mushroom cloud since Hiroshima but we haven't blown ourselves up yet, and I don't think there's going to be a worldwide flood either. Climate change is just climate change; the planet's getting warmer like it did eons ago. Then it'll get colder again. The whole thing's natural and humanity will adjust to it."

"Are you saying the Change didn't change anything?"

"Sure it did," said Jack. "No change occurs in isolation. Each one no matter how small has a ripple effect, and change itself is a constant. It's like the universe, always in motion. Looking to the future, we thought robotics and artificial intelligence were what we had to worry about. Would there be enough jobs, would we be replaced by thinking machines? We were right to worry but we sure as hell worried about the wrong things."

"Don't we always?" Tilbury asked.

Silence seeped into the room like a living presence. They could feel its effect in the atmosphere, the chill of the unknown.

The Change seemed a lifetime away. A mild annoyance they would welcome back in exchange for . . .

For what?

Jack's gaze wandered to Nell Bennett, who was looking down at her left hand.

She was wearing the square-cut emerald Jack had bought for her in Arthur Hannisch's jewelry shop. The glowing green stone was not perfectly clear; in its depths were the leaflike shadows called *jardin,* or gardens. Emeralds were the only precious gems whose imperfections were considered a virtue.

Nell and Jack had never completed their fateful wedding ceremony, but later he had insisted on slipping the ring onto her finger anyway. Looking into the depths of the jewel was like looking into the Garden of Eden. Nell could pretend to herself that in spite of life's flaws, everything would be all right. Someday.

On this evening several rounds of drinks and a gallant effort at conviviality failed to lift the somber mood. The gathering broke up earlier than usual. As Gerry's passengers returned to the horse-bus he caught Jack by the arm. "I'd like to take another look at your car if that's okay."

"Sure, but why? Do you think you know what caused the damage?"

"That's just it, I don't know, but science must have the answer. A friend of mine's a metallurgist who lives over in Benning; I'd like him to examine it."

"Bring him out to Bud's, then, I'll meet him there. If he has an answer I'm sure we'd both like to hear it."

Erasmus Barber did not look like Jack's mental image of a metallurgist. When Gerry brought him to Moriarty's Garage a week later, Jack thought the man resembled a genetically modified stork: very tall, very thin, with a nose like a beak and outsized hands on womanly wrists. His watery blue eyes appeared to be climbing out of the heavy bags beneath them.

Bud Moriarty did not welcome his arrival. As Jack told Bea Fontaine, "The two circled each other like two alpha dogs with their hackles raised. I guess Bud resented having 'an expert' brought onto his patch. He likes to think of himself as the expert when it comes to cars, but Barber told him a lot he didn't know."

The metallurgist had gingerly eased down into the pit, where he could observe the distorted car from different angles. When he started to apply a chisel to one fender Jack protested. Gerry pointed out, "He can't do more damage than you've got already."

The chisel wasn't necessary. The metal surrendered to the first touch of the man's fingers. As if he were peeling fruit, Barber methodically removed pieces of the Mustang and arranged them on the floor of the garage. He went from one to another, constantly muttering. Each scrap was given a spell of undivided attention. His low monotone was a conversation he held only with himself.

Watching, waiting, the other men exchanged small talk. Sports, weather, nothing important enough to be distracting. No mention of the Baltic.

Lacey brought a hamper of tuna sandwiches without mayonnaise and a large thermos of artificially sweetened iced tea. She spread a tablecloth beside the pit and set out a picnic. Bud dutifully helped himself to sandwiches and tea, but after a taste or two both Gerry and Jack decided to wait for a more satisfying lunch elsewhere.

At last Barber brushed off his hands with an air of finality. "Mr. Reece, is this car supposed to be authentic?"

Jack bristled. "It is authentic."

"I'm afraid not. Do you know how the molded steel body of your car was manufactured?"

"Sure."

Barber said, "I wonder if you do. When we began to forge metal we were teaching ourselves to alter basic matter. No other creature on the planet does that." He was unaware that as he spoke, the romance he felt for the topic colored his voice. "For example, when iron is repeatedly heated and manipulated a small amount of carbon is left behind; more than occurred in the original smelting process. That additional carbon acts on the atoms of iron and turns the material to steel.

"The Eiffel Tower in Paris was built of wrought iron in the late nineteenth century, shortly before steel became the metal of choice for building. Within a few years steel frameworks supported every metropolitan skyline. Unfortunately structural steel begins to sustain damage at six hundred degrees Fahrenheit, as New York tragically discovered on 9/11.

"Other supportive materials are now being employed, like cement, or even glass, but steel is still essential to industry. There are many types of steel. Depending on its intended usage, steel can be alloyed with elements like magnesium, chromium, nickel or niobium to provide properties like shininess or resistance to oxidation. Without manganese, steel would break up during further heat treatment. And without a number of other alloys the space station and our satellites would be impossible.

"I don't know who sold you this piece of junk you call a car but it's very low-alloy; something strategic is lacking, Mr. Reece. I couldn't say what the missing element is without an X-ray, but there's about as much cohesion here as damp cardboard. You claim you've actually been driving around in this . . . this incomplete thing?"

"I sure have; for years!"

Erasmus Barber rolled his eyes heavenward. "You must have a guardian angel working overtime."

*The Sycamore Seed* did not carry an item about the vandalism of Jack Reece's car. Lila Ragland had considered writing one but it would have to pass scrutiny by Frank Auerbach, publisher and editor of the newspaper, and she knew what he would say. "I'm paying you to be an investigative reporter, Lila. If you can find out who and what caused the damage you can have a column for it, but otherwise just give me a human interest story to counter the bad news from the Baltic. I want my paper to give its readers balance."

There should be an easier way to make a living, Lila thought, than writing for a small-town newspaper.

Before the demise of the internet she had enjoyed a very different, and much easier, source of income. Born to an unmarried woman who lived on the wrong side of the river and made her living servicing men, Lila Ragland had escaped her squalid background as soon as she was old enough. She had spent years educating herself. Beauty and brains took her far. A virtuoso at hacking, she had learned to extract other people's money from their bank accounts without a shred of conscience. When she returned to Sycamore River she expected to be able to live the kind of life she had dreamed of as a child.

Instead her homecoming had coincided with the onset of the Change. Cyber crime was on its way out.

It was sheer luck that Edgar Tilbury had taken pity on her and become her mentor.

"I feel a bit like a chameleon," she once confessed to him. He knew her story—or as much as she was willing to confide to anyone. "I was someone very different once, but I'm an honest woman now with an honest job. And I'm happy about it." She had sounded a little defensive.

"You don't have to work for a living, didn't your grandfather leave you all those bank shares?"

"Bank shares." Lila's laughter was hollow. "Lots of things aren't what they seem, Edgar. I didn't know Oliver Staunton was my grandfather until after he was dead and they found his will. The bank shares he left me aren't worth the paper they were printed on."

The Sycamore and Staunton Mercantile Bank had been one of the many casualties of the Change.

*The Sycamore Seed* had survived the Change due to the insatiable human appetite to know what was happening. As wallscreens and the internet failed, only the few working AllComs supplied the daily news. Then newspapers that had been almost extinct began to make a comeback. Modern printing machinery had capitulated to the Change, but Frank Auerbach had scoured the Sycamore River Valley until he located enough discarded machines in basements and junkyards to assemble a press that could produce readable print, though the ink tended to smear.

Lila Ragland's job was likely to be secure for some time to come.

Edgar Tilbury's extensive library included several sets of encyclopedias printed in real books and not microengraved on glass discs. Lila had unearthed all the information she could find about nuclear weapons, condensed it into readable copy, then condensed it again until *The Sycamore Seed* could bring out a special edition.

Frank Auerbach had refused at first. "This is scare mongering, Lila; it's worse than giving the rising sea levels. I feel a sense of responsibility to our readers."

"So do I! They can't jump on the net anymore and find out what they need to know. I think the schools should initiate bomb drills like they did during the Second World War. There's no good reason to withhold information from people who should be prepared." As she spoke she was thinking of Edgar Tilbury.

"Maybe you're right," Auerbach said. "Maybe . . . I just don't want to face it."

"You'd rather wake up to a nasty surprise when it's too late to do anything about it?"

The *Seed* put out a special edition.

Like ripples from a flung stone, Sunnyslope Cemetery began receiving inquiries about grave sites for sale.

# 4

Erasmus Barber was getting inquiries too. Jack Reece's car was not the only man-made object to suffer a sudden and inexplicable collapse. It was not even the first. Not in the town, the state, or the country.

Not in the world.

Here and there—but not everywhere, and not all at once—the essential structure of metal objects was being altered. Little things at first; the Ford Mustang was an exception. Most were inconsequential items whose loss was only an annoyance, hardly worth mentioning.

Neighbors began coming to the metallurgist's door seeking an explanation for softened doorknobs that could not be turned and drawer pulls that fell off in their hands.

"I don't know what to tell them," he complained to his wife, whom he called Sweetie. Maybelline Barber was named for her grandmother, who had been given the title of a popular song no one remembered anymore. Both of the Barbers had suffered throughout their schooldays from the burden of silly names. It was the first thing they discovered they had in common.

"If there's trouble with the metal, Razz, it's not your fault," his wife consoled him. "The blame lies with the manufacturer."

"But the same one didn't make the doorknobs *and* the drawer pulls. You didn't see that car in Sycamore River, Sweetie; it was the same way too. The metal was flabby, almost gritty. I could draw a line in it with my finger. The man who owned the car was really upset and so was his mechanic. I explained to them about alloys but it didn't satisfy them. Didn't satisfy me either, to be honest. I asked to take a sample to the laboratory over in Nolan's Falls, but that mechanic thought I was trying to get away with something."

Her eyes flashed. "You wouldn't do that!"

"You know it and I know it, Sweetie, but it's not something you can prove to strangers. And he was right not to trust me; I slipped a piece into my pocket when no one was looking."

"What explanation are you giving our friends with the doorknobs?"

"The plain truth," Barber replied. "Which is: I don't know."

"Tell them that, then. Lord knows we've got more worries than soft doorknobs. The news these days is full of war; when will it be, will America be attacked, is someone going to drop The Bomb . . ." Her eyes filled with tears. "I'm scared, Razz. It's like waiting for the end of the world."

Barber folded his wife into his arms. "I guess it's a good thing we're not young anymore, Sweetie. With any luck we won't live to see it."

———

Threats of impending war were having their effect on Nell Bennett, though she tried to keep her disquiet from her son and daughter. Jess paid little attention to the news, being more interested in boys; she recently had begun a relationship with Evan Mulligan. He often rode his chestnut mare, Rocket, to their house and tied her to one of the trees out front while he and Jess talked upstairs in her room.

Nell was certain they did more than talk, but Jess was old enough and she certainly knew to take precautions. On the one occasion when her mother had questioned her about the subject she acted insulted. For several days the atmosphere between the two women had been frosty. When it finally normalized Nell managed to avoid setting things off again. But she mourned the loss of her little girl.

Colin presented a different problem. A sturdy, square-shouldered youngster who looked more mature than he really was, he resembled his late father in appearance but not in temperament. He was sensitive and imaginative, a dreamer by nature. Throughout his childhood he had been enthralled by war games played on the computer. To him they were heart-poundingly real. Nell had thought they were a juvenile pastime until the day a casual conversation revealed that most of his opponents were adults.

Many did not even live in America.

"Do they realize they're gaming with children?" Nell demanded to know.

"I'm not a child!" her son had flared.

"There are predators who use the internet to gain access to vulnerable people of any age, Colin. I understand they can be very persuasive. Perhaps we should install a monitoring system on your computer."

"You do that," he had retorted hotly, "and I'll go online at a friend's house. Don't you trust me to have any sense?"

Since then the demise of the internet had rendered the problem irrelevant, but the question of trust had become a permanent minefield. Nell had decided to give both children a chance; the alternative might be to lose them altogether. As a result she found herself living with two individuals who were related to her yet no longer part of her. Any reference to personal relationships or current events had to be passed through her mental filter first.

Conversations in the Bennett household became boringly superficial.

Colin considered the international conflict that was brewing as an improved version of the war games he had loved, played out on a larger scale. He avidly followed the political negotiations on the wallscreen but balked at the idea of going to college. "I don't want to spend years sitting in a classroom getting calluses on my backside." If the boy's father were still alive he would have forced Colin to get a higher education, even if he had to break his spirit to do it, but Nell was not like Robert Bennett. She just wanted her children to be happy.

While Colin was waiting for an unidentified adventure to appear on his horizon, he took a job at Deel's Hardware. The work was physical but not difficult, and allowed him plenty of time for daydreaming. Occasionally he showed a flash of the ambition that had motivated Robert Bennett by making suggestions to his boss, who usually ignored them.

Nell was surprised when he came home from work one day and announced, "I'm thinking of enlisting."

"What are you talking about? You're too young."

"I am now, but my birthday's in five months. The recruitment officer down at the center said if I enlist then instead of waiting for the draft, I'll have a better chance of getting the service I want. A lot of the guys are doing it; it beats the hell out of going to rust in this sleepy town."

"Does he think there will be a draft?"

"Oh yeah," Colin replied nonchalantly. "If there's going to be conventional warfare there'll be a draft; how else could they fill out the infantry? If it's nuclear, though, and he seemed pretty sure it would be, they'll need people to train in robotics and that would suit me just fine."

"Robotics?" Nell was still trying to absorb the idea of her son's enlisting.

"For the drones," Colin said with the barely concealed exasperation of a man forced to explain the obvious. "We've got more drones than the other side, the unmanned kind that carry nuclear warheads. They'll be fighting the real war. When the recruitment officer learned I was Robert Bennett's son he was dead impressed. 'We might have something special for you,' he told me. He called his superior officer in to talk to me and they gave me a stack of forms to fill out. When the war gets going I'll be in the thick of everything."

The next time she saw Jack, Nell told him about the conversation. "Colin was boasting to me," she said, "about having a military career. Killing people."

"Don't blame yourself for it."

"I don't; I blame those wretched war games he used to play. If only the computers had failed before—"

"It wasn't the fault of computer games, Nell; at least not entirely. Face it; ours is an aggressive species. The male more than the female, perhaps, but it's in our genes; that's why we're at the top of the food chain. You can't change biology.

"In recent decades there's been a move in America to introduce men to the female side of their natures, to make them more nurturing and caring, but it isn't a total success. There's a lot of hidden resentment bubbling away under the surface, which tends to screw up the balance between the sexes. Some anthropologists claim we're descended from carnivorous chimpanzees, the so-called killer apes, which is why we . . ."

Too late he realized that his rather pompous discourse might have reminded Nell of her relationship with her deceased husband.

Her chin came up. "Rob was not *all* bad," she said icily.

In that moment he felt her slip another inch away from him.

When will I learn not to lecture people? Probably never, it's part of me.

On the following night there was a full moon, one of the so-called super moons beloved of photographers. Jack took Nell to dinner at their favorite restaurant. His new car had been purchased only that morning; not an amphibian, it was strictly a land model looking hopefully toward the future. It was a marine blue coupé with a blunt nose in front and a fantail behind. When the first of its model appeared in Sycamore River a local wag had remarked, "Looks like a giant bird rushing away after running into a brick wall."

In the showroom Jack had been eager to look under the hood, once he discovered how to raise it. What he found were rubber pipes that doubled back on themselves and a configuration of shafts and blades twisted like the propeller of an airplane.

"She's a great little sports car, sir," the salesman had enthused. He prided himself on being a good judge of character. "Just the thing for a man like you. Look here on the control panel, what used to be called the dashboard, and press *this,* and there you are! On that screen you have a complete diagnostic of your engine, all the info you need to know. The button here is for your VC, which advises you where the nearest charge point is. She's got a really sexy voice, but we can always change it if your wife—"

"I don't have a wife."

The salesman gave Jack a broad wink. "Don't s'pose you'd like to take mine along with the car? I'd give you a good deal on her. One woman, hardly used and still in running order."

"I'll be doing good to afford the car by itself. Is the sticker price correct?"

"It is. And you're looking at the last car you can get for that. If and when they get here the next lot's going to cost at least another thousand."

"The hell you say! For the same car? What a ripoff."

"It's not my fault," the salesman protested. "The manufacturer's had a delay on the assembly line; something about the metal being faulty. I don't understand the technical details but factories all over the country are complaining. The *Wall Street Journal's* warning of a possible shutdown of heavy industry."

Jack hoped it was not just a sales pitch, but he had bought the blue coupé. Half an hour had passed during which his credit details were checked and authorized, then there was another wait while his thumbprint recognition template was imprinted into the car's ignition system. At last he had slid into the driver's seat.

The soft leather conformed to his body shape.

On the drive home Jack had stopped several times to change settings and consult the screen. He was intrigued to see that every revolution of the wheels had made a minuscule difference. The controls might have come off the bridge of a spaceship. He began to take pride in his purchase. Mustang was the past; he was driving the future.

When Nell saw the car her only comment was, "That's nice."

"You don't like it?"

"It's a car, Jack; what do you want me to say? I'm not a car person."

"You liked the Mustang."

"Well, it was red and I like red."

For once there was no threat of rain. The flame of the setting sun was extinguished by a sky soon paved with stars. As they drove into town Jack recalled Nell sitting beside him in his convertible, wearing a pale chiffon scarf on her hair and designer sunglasses, looking like a film star. Only a year ago but it seemed longer than that.

She would learn to love the new car too. Give her time.

The restaurant was crowded and they had to wait for a table. When they attempted casual conversation it sounded forced. There were awkward pauses while each tried to think of something that would be interesting to the other.

If it hadn't been for the Change, Jack said to himself. But everything changes. We might have been happily married by now. Or we might already be on the sorry road that leads to married couples in a restaurant not talking, just staring into space. All the magic lost. Isn't it better to find out beforehand?

"Isn't it?" he unintentionally said aloud.

Nell looked up from her salade Niçoise. "Isn't it what?"

Thinking fast, he swept his eyes around the room. "Isn't it sad how many people don't look as if they're having a good time?" His gaze returned to her. "What about you? Are you enjoying yourself?"

"'Enjoying yourself' sounds like masturbating," she replied. She laughed at his nonplussed expression. "I guess that wasn't the answer you hoped for."

"Not exactly. I'm surprised, that's all." In their intimate moments Nell could be delightfully uninhibited, but otherwise she had what Sycamore River called "old money manners." Her remark seemed out of character with his vision of her.

"C'mon, Jack, I'm not a prude."

"I know that. You're everything I want in a woman."

"My, aren't we getting serious!"

"These are serious times. The threat of war . . ."

She put her hand on his. The hand with the emerald. "It's more than a threat, isn't it?"

If Jack knew one thing for sure about Nell it was that she insisted on honesty, a quality he usually considered negotiable. He was inclined to tell people what they wanted to hear; "greasing the wheels," he called it. But with Nell clutching his hand he had no choice. "If I were a racing man I'd call it a dead cert." Leaning forward, he added, "I want us to go ahead and get married now, right now. Tonight if we could;

we still have the license. Let's start living our lives while we still have lives to live."

"You're scaring me."

"I mean to. Every day is somebody's last day."

The soft planes of her face seemed to alter almost imperceptibly. Became stronger. "That future you're dismissing so casually belongs to my children, Jack; to Jess and Colin and all the other young people. I refuse to surrender a day of it to a lunatic with a God complex and his finger on the nuclear button!" She was briefly incandescent with passion.

Joan of Arc might have looked like that, Jack thought, when she rode out to have Charles crowned the king of France. Catch the moment right now and hold on to it, it's not going to get any better than this. "You're beautiful," he said aloud.

"And you're changing the subject." She brought her wineglass to her lips but put it back on the table, untasted. Her eyes gazed into the middle distance. "Maybe I'm just not ready to be rushed into marriage."

"Hardly rushed," he pointed out. "We've been planning it for months."

"Those plans were based on circumstances that have changed now. You said it yourself: the threat of war. Colin's talking about enlisting and he's still . . . well, he may be old enough to have a job in a hardware store but he's not ready to fight a war, he only thinks he is. I should have put my foot down with him long ago; he wouldn't accept it from me now.

It's the same with Jess. I want to protect her, but somewhere along the line I've ceased being the parent. I didn't feel it happen and there's no going back. I'm losing control of my life, Jack."

"Then let me help you."

"Male chauvinist," she accused with a smile that crinkled her eyes at the corners. She did not want her expression to give her feelings away. Nell had gone straight from her parents to her marriage; until now, there had been no period in her life when she alone was responsible for herself. She was reluctant to surrender her autonomy.

Nell lowered her lashes and watched her recently manicured fingers pleating the napkin on her lap. "Between Rob's insurance and what the government paid me for the RobBenn land I have enough money, and my children are too old to need a father figure. So why should we marry? These days people don't have to be married to live together. They don't even have to belong to opposite sexes. You could move in with me, Jack; there's plenty of room."

"I don't want to live in Robert Bennett's house and I can't afford the kind of house you deserve."

"That's foolish pride speaking."

"You don't love me," he accused.

"Now you're trying to manipulate me."

They finished the meal in silence. Each was thinking the same thing: maybe marriage would be a mistake.

When their eyes met they both looked away.

Usually Jack ordered dessert; the restaurant was famous for its Black Forest cheesecake. This time he wasn't hungry.

Nor did Nell request her favorite lemon sherbet.

"Are you in a hurry to get home?" he asked.

"Mmm." No answer, just a noncommittal hum.

If the romance was cooling, something perverse in Jack resolved to hang on. To spin out their time together he ordered two brandies, confident that Nell would never refuse a nightcap. It was part of the hardwired pattern for a proper upbringing, like saying please and thank you.

She smiled politely when their drinks arrived but only touched her lips to the brandy. She put the full snifter down on the table. Folded her napkin on her plate, picked up her handbag, smoothed her skirts and glanced meaningfully toward the door.

Jack took the hint.

The full moon was beaming down on Jack's new car as it waited in the parking lot. Part of him still expected to see the red Mustang. The blue coupé looked out of place, like an unfamiliar prop intended for someone else's life. He experienced the same disassociation he had felt riding on the hay wagon with Edgar Tilbury. As if they were other people.

He shrugged to throw it off.

"You all right?"

"Fine, Nell. Just fine."

They had almost reached the car when an unexpected movement caught Jack's attention. He glanced up. A shapeless cloud of pale violet light hung over the parking lot. The cloud drifted slowly, sweeping from left to right like a blind hand searching. Wherever it encountered a high point a torch of brightness bloomed, then vanished with a crackling noise.

Jack stopped in his tracks. "Saint Elmo's fire?"

Nell followed the direction of his gaze. "What's that?"

"A discharge of atmospheric electricity; sometimes it appears at sea or on the wings of airplanes. I've seen it before but never in that form. The color reminds me of something else . . ." Narrowing his eyes, Jack spotted a dark object hovering above the tarmac. It was roughly three feet long, ovoid in shape but narrowing at both ends.

The violet light approached and enveloped the dark object. Paused. Flowed on.

There was a smell of ozone in the air.

When the light moved in their direction Jack reached for Nell and roughly pulled her behind him.

She tried to push his hands away. "What do you think you're doing!"

"Don't let that light touch you."

"How could it possibly hurt me?" She sounded annoyed.

As the violet light reached them it gave a startled jump the way a living person might do—and winked out.

The night was eerily quiet.

# 5

Jack bundled Nell into the car and began working the control panel. The door locks operated with a satisfying click. An almost silent mechanical response heralded the start of the engine; concealed exterior panels opened and headlights sprang to life.

When a honeyed female voice asked for his destination Jack growled, "I don't know, just get us out of here."

The coupé left the parking lot at top speed, wheels spitting gravel. After several blocks Nell twisted in her seat to peer out the rear window. "I don't see that light anywhere now."

"Maybe we weren't meant to see it."

"Why not?"

"I don't know. It looked like it was searching for something. There was a drone above the parking lot, maybe that's what the light was after."

"Were we in any danger?"

"The light didn't seem to be interested in us, but none of this makes much sense. Who flies drones at night?"

"Whoever it is, I don't like being spied on!"

"The drone could belong to our military," Jack speculated, "and be used for reconnaissance. But what did the light have to do with it? Maybe it wasn't even ours. Years ago there was concern that our enemies might use an electromagnetic pulse against us and destroy the national grid. It never happened and everyone forgot about it, but a weapon like that might make use of light in some way."

Nell shuddered. "The whole thing's decidedly spooky."

"We're living in yesterday's future," said Jack. "Today there are a lot of scientific advances the man on the street might call 'spooky.'"

"That certainly applies to drones and purple lights! We went out for a pleasant evening and stumbled into this. I don't like it, I feel invaded. You still haven't told me why our military would reconnoiter a town like Sycamore River."

"The shape of our country's changing, Nell. Some of the East Coast's under water now; remember the latest pictures from New York? Parts of the city look like Venice. The sea's coming this way; the skeptics who refused to believe in global warming are going to have to take swimming lessons. The drone we saw may have been helping to update the maps."

"This far inland? At night?"

He did not have an answer.

She clenched her fists in her lap. The miles sped by. When she spoke her voice was not quite steady. "Did you mean what you said about getting married tomorrow?"

"I did. Do."

"Let me think about it overnight and then talk to Jess and Colin. I don't know about tomorrow, but maybe . . ."

"Of course," Jack replied. He knew he sounded distracted but couldn't help it. Part of his mind was occupied with wondering if what they had seen could be credited to a hostile power. If so, was that power responsible for the drone? Or for the light?

An attack might be closer than anyone realized.

Their farewell embrace at her front door was perfunctory. Jack drove home with a hollow feeling in the pit of his stomach.

He found Bea Fontaine already in bed, propped against a mountain of pillows and reading a detective novel. Apollo was curled up beside her, a mountain of orange fur rumbling with contentment. He lifted his head to regard the interloper with hostile yellow eyes.

When Jack's aunt saw the expression on his face she marked her place with a bookmark depicting the Acropolis, and set the book aside. "Push Apollo out of the way and sit down here by me. Now . . . what's wrong?"

He told her what he had seen. "The drone wasn't big enough to carry a person, Aunt Bea, and as far as I could tell there were no markings on it. In the dark it was hard to be sure. It may have been made of aluminum coated with something that renders it invisible to radar, like the old Stealth Bombers. The whole thing was damned suspicious, anyhow."

"The light you saw; did it come from the drone?"

"I honestly don't know. But when it went off I suspect the information had already been transmitted to whoever sent the drone; by radio waves, perhaps. It's no technology I'm familiar with. And I'm not sure it has a benign purpose."

"Dear God, Jack!"

"As soon as I left Nell at home I called the military base in Trenton. I know people there, and I made some inquiries."

"And?"

"What I heard wasn't reassuring. They asked for specific details and told me not to mention it to anyone else."

"So you're telling me."

"I didn't think you'd run out into the street shouting the news."

"Not in my nightgown; no." Suddenly cold, Bea pulled the bedclothes around her shoulders. Apollo growled at being disturbed a second time. Bea said, "Before the internet went down social media would have been buzzing with information about this. As it is . . . will the government tell us what's going on?"

"They didn't try to keep the explosion in the Baltic a secret."

"That was too big to conceal, Jack; like an earthquake. Drones spying on us for a foreign power is something else. For all we know America could be at war already and we'll only find out when it's too late. But why would our enemies want to attack Sycamore River? There's nothing here, no heavy industry, not even a major rail hub anymore. The

Change shrunk us back into an old-fashioned town that's no threat to anybody."

"It's an old-fashioned town that's centrally located," Jack said, "at the confluence of several rivers. A nuclear attack here could affect millions, particularly if the prevailing winds were right. And there's a sizeable airport at Nolan's Falls; that might be a target too if they have any military planes there.

"Tell me something, Aunt Bea. Did Edgar Tilbury ever tell you about his bolt-hole? Is it some kind of bomb shelter?"

"I wouldn't put too much store in those tall tales of his, Jack. Edgar's reached the age where some men remember a past that never happened."

"He said Lila knew about it."

"Ask her, then."

Jack watched his aunt's fingers gently massaging the base of Apollo's ears. The cat's purr rose to a thunderous volume. "If there is a bomb shelter," Bea said thoughtfully, "I wonder if he'd let animals in?"

The following morning Jack awoke even earlier than usual. A soon as he was dressed he went out on the front porch and looked up and down the street, the almost unchanged street of his boyhood. He did not know what he had expected to find but was relieved by the familiarity of every house and tree.

The breakfast Bea prepared for him was familiar too, and

the waffles tasted . . . right. Yet he could not shake off the expectation of . . . what?

When he went out to the garage and slid into the driver's seat of the coupé he discovered a tiny purple light glowing on the control panel, informing him the car had updated its software overnight. The unexpected light was unsettling.

Jack pressed the button marked VA. "Only show the software light if I request it," he instructed.

His first stop of the morning was at the offices of *The Sycamore Seed*. "Offices" was a misnomer; the newspaper was published in a cavernous red brick building that had once housed a cattle market. Now the business and editorial departments as well as the printing machinery shared a space which, on a hot day, emitted a faint whiff of cow manure.

The town had long since exhausted all the possible jokes.

When Jack came in, Frank Auerbach was sitting at the front desk; a small rumpled man wearing a rumpled brown suit, with the sleeves of the jacket pushed up to his elbows. His watery eyes were like poached eggs trying to climb out of the bags beneath them.

He greeted Jack by saying, "Whaddaya think of this?" He held up a sheet of advertising copy on which an airbrushed model who was naked from the waist up proclaimed *GOET-TINGER'S PREDICTS MINOAN STYLE IS THE NEW LOOK!*

"That's for page three?" Jack guessed.

"Nah, it goes opposite the weather forecast; the department store says women check the weather before they go shopping."

"I predict young girls will look great in it," Jack said, "and grown women will look delusional."

Auerbach laughed. "You got a hot news item for us, or are you ordering a subscription?"

"My aunt subscribes to the *Seed* and I read hers."

"Cheapskate. If all the people who read this newspaper would buy their own—"

"Crocodiles would sing soprano, Frank. Is Lila here?"

Auerbach gave a nod toward the rear of the building. "Her desk is the one on the left, beside the back door."

"Why'd you put her so far from the front?"

"Lemme tell you something. I'm fifty-nine years old, I got high blood pressure and a peptic ulcer and my wife's beginning to look like my mother-in-law. But when I turn around and watch Lila Ragland walking to her desk, just for a minute I'm twenty again. Y'know what I mean?"

Jack grinned. "I know exactly what you mean. She's not really what you'd call beautiful, but if we could bottle what Lila has we could make a fortune."

"You here to see her? I thought you were seeing Eleanor Bennett."

"I need to discuss something with Lila if she's not too busy. Say, do you know anything more about the explosion in the Baltic?"

"Nothing we haven't printed. We got it off the wire and after that . . ." Auerbach held out his empty hands, palm up.

"What do you mean, 'after that'?"

"After that nothing, the next item that came through was totally unrelated, and that's how it's been ever since. Media silence. Lila's been trying to substantiate the story but no luck. Maybe it was a hoax."

"Maybe," Jack said in an even tone.

A couple of minutes later Lila agreed with his skepticism. "That news flash slipped through by mistake and was denied almost at once," she told him. "It often happens to reports from that part of the world. Without the World Wide Web it's like we're half blind."

"Edgar Tilbury thinks losing the Web was a blessing."

"Edgar's an opinionated curmudgeon. But he's my curmudgeon and I'm fond of him; when I came back to Sycamore River he was my first friend."

"I assume he's offered you a place in his bomb shelter if things go pear-shaped?"

"He's talked to you about the shelter?"

"Only in passing; he said you could tell me about it if I was interested. Does he really have one, Lila?"

"He has one all right, and it's probably the next best thing to being under Cheyenne Mountain. It began with a single hole in the ground. Edgar wanted to bury something on the side of a hill but then he kept on digging. He can be obsessive once he gets going. He opened up a central chamber and several tunnels, reinforced them and added all sorts of refinements. He says it wouldn't withstand a direct nuclear hit but it's strong enough to resist almost anything else."

"How many people could it hold comfortably? And for how long?"

"How long would depend on the duration of the emergency. As for how many, that's anyone's guess. Edgar's land is on limestone; it's honeycombed with caves he discovered when he started digging. He figures the whole area was part of an underground river system ages ago."

"Is there any standing water in it now?"

"I told you, it's on a hill, well above the water table. But he's installed pumps just in case. Edgar's careful about things like that."

"How about provisions?"

"He's got shelves and storerooms chock-full of nonperishables. Lots of pasta, for example; Edgar's a fiend for pasta. Any items that won't last for more than a month he replaces on a regular basis."

Jack gave a low whistle. "I'm impressed. And surprised that he's willing for people to know about it."

"Not people, Jack; just a few friends. 'Folks he wouldn't mind being cooped up with' is the way he puts it. If he told you about his bolt-hole he must think we're going to need it pretty soon."

"What do you think?"

Lila met his eyes squarely. "I'm afraid he's right. Look at this item we took off the wire this morning." She retrieved a manila folder from her desk. Her hands were shaking slightly as she handed the folder to him. The contents spilled onto the floor in an avalanche of typed transcripts and paper clips.

Jack crouched to pick them up.

What he saw were not paper clips.

Lying on the bare floor were small silvery wires twisted into bizarre shapes.

An echo of his own words sounded in Jack's head. *It looked like a giant had crumpled the Mustang in his hands.*

"What the hell are these, Lila?"

"Paper clips. You know, they hold pages together." She took one from his fingers and turned it over in hers.

"Do you have any more?"

"Sure. In my desk." She opened the center drawer of the gray steel desk and took out a pasteboard box with no lid. The box was half full of paper clips. Ordinary paper clips.

"Is this where you got them from?" he asked.

"Certainly."

"When did you take them out?"

"A little while ago."

"And they were okay then?"

"Of course they were, Jack, and they're okay now."

He stared at her. "You don't see . . . I mean I get these hunches . . ." He had started to say "visions" but stopped himself. The word carried a connotation that would be misleading. "They happen very rarely and they aren't exactly hunches; more like a warning. Something simply isn't *right*. It's as if another world is overlaying this one; similar but not the same. Blurring the lines. It's damned unpleasant."

"And you've got one of those hunches about paper clips? I always thought you were a hardheaded realist."

"I am, Lila, but even a realist knows there are more things in this world than can be observed with only five senses. A common housefly with its multifaceted eyes can see a whole spectrum of colors that humans are blind to."

She gave him a measuring look. "Don't take this the wrong way, but I suggest you talk to Gloria Delmonico."

"I'm not losing my mind. Maybe I've retained an atavistic instinct; our ancient ancestors probably knew when a saber-toothed tiger was waiting outside the cave. It happened to me before the Change and it's happening again." Jack struggled to convey his idea. "Your paper clips are a clue that our world . . . or an aspect of our world . . . is becoming unstable."

She looked at the clip in her hand. The ordinary paper clip. "I don't know what you're talking about."

He realized he was asking Lila to take a step outside of reality and it was a step too far. No words of his would be sufficient to give access to what was happening inside his head. "Forget it," he said abruptly. "I'm just rambling; too much on my mind, I guess. I came to ask you about Edgar's bomb shelter because I want Nell to see it. We may get married soon after all."

"That's wonderful, Jack! I still have my dress for the wedding that never happened."

"Buy a new one," he advised. "For luck."

# 6

Sycamore River dozed in the golden sunshine of a late autumn; light without heat, but at least a break from the summer's constant storms. The town's inhabitants were thankful for the change in the weather. After the Change they had begun to resume normal lives with an almost postwar euphoria, though they were aware another war might be around the corner. But that was in the uncharted land called The Future. It might never come.

For now the schools were open, offices and shops were busy. The petty annoyances of ordinary lives—the domestic quarrels and health problems and unpaid bills—occupied center stage.

Clarence Deel, ordering winter stock for his hardware store, had compiled an order that would delight his wholesalers. Colin Bennett questioned just how many snow shovels the store could expect to sell. "What if we don't get any blizzards this year?" he asked his employer.

"Don't be ridiculous, we always have a blizzard in January if not before. You clear out those front windows and get them ready for a new display and let me make the decisions; I've been doing it just fine for thirty years."

That night Deel told his wife, "The Bennett kid's getting too big for his britches. He's trying to tell me how to run my business."

"His whole family thinks they shit pearls," she sneered. "Eleanor Bennett came into my salon the other day for a cut and blow-dry and kept nattering on about having another wedding, but she never bothered to invite me."

"She marrying the same man as before?"

"I think so."

"Some people never learn," Deel muttered.

"What's that supposed to mean?"

"She didn't invite you to the other wedding either. You should be thankful, you missed being a witness to murder."

"That won't happen again."

"Maybe not, but it's an unlucky family all the same."

"Then you shouldn't have hired that boy to work for you. What if his bad luck rubs off on you?"

"It won't. I've told you a hundred times there's no such thing as 'bad luck,' woman. I think I'll have Colin work on weekends for a while, just to show him who's boss."

"What if he enlists?"

"I don't think he's old enough. Anyway, he's more talk than action."

"This time we're not going to be married in a chapel," Nell told her mother. "I don't want to do anything the way we did before. A registry office, that's all we need, and maybe a bottle of champagne after."

Katharine Richmond had a strong sense of the proprieties. "What about your attendants?"

"You're the mother of the bride and Lila Ragland will be my bridesmaid. Edgar Tilbury will stand up with Jack."

"He's not an old friend."

"He's old and he's a friend, Mom; besides, he's a member of the Wednesday Club. I think you should get to know him."

"Why would I want to? He's not—"

"Not like us, is that what you were going to say? A person has to meet your high standards to be worth knowing? The only man you thought was good enough to marry me was the worst possible husband I could've had, but he was like us, he came from the right background and went to the right schools. And he made my life hell. Thank you so much!"

Her mother was shocked at the outburst. "Why, *Eleanor!*"

Once they had opened, Nell could not seem to close her emotional floodgates. "We're on the verge of war right now; war with people who basically are the same as us but speak a different language and have a different worldview. They'd probably look down their noses at *you* and do their best to exterminate you. What everybody needs right now is an attitude adjustment!"

When Jack rang her AllCom later, Nell told him about the quarrel. "I don't know what got into me, I've never lost my temper like that with her." The face on the screen of the All-Com looked contrite.

"Maybe it was long overdue. Did you feel better afterward?"

"No, but I'm glad I did it just the same."


Patricia Staunton Nyeberger, wife of Dwayne Nyeberger and daughter of the late president of the bank, had been murdered by a stranger in the eruption of random violence that accompanied the Change in Sycamore River. Subsequently her husband had gone on a rampage of his own and been killed by the local sheriff, leaving the five Nyeberger boys orphaned.

There was adequate money in the family estate to hire a staff and finish raising the boys in the home they had always known. The oldest, Sandy, was eighteen, and should have been able to take some responsibility for his siblings. Had the family involved been less well connected there might have been legal objections to the arrangement. As it was, the objections were personal.

"I've had it," Gloria Delmonico complained to the chief of staff of the Hilda Staunton Memorial Hospital. "I cannot spend another afternoon trying to turn those savages into human beings. Sandy's as out of control as the younger ones; they have no idea how to behave. After three hours with them I go home and shout at my own family and I don't mean to."

Mitchell Congreve was sympathetic, but he had only recently been appointed chief of staff and was very aware of small-town politics. "We don't have anyone else as qualified as you are to help them, Gloria. Remember all they've been through."

"I know, I think about it every time I look at poor Kirby; his face is badly scarred and his two hands are like claws. All five still have nightmares about the explosion and fire at Rob-Benn, but Kirby's also having nightmares about his plastic surgery. He'll be grown long before it's finished, if it ever is finished. And he was such a beautiful little boy!

"But Mitch . . . I mean, Chief, I'm still getting used to that . . . there's more to the job than I expected and I'm not sure I *am* qualified. The staff at the Staunton house is like a revolving door. New nurses and housekeepers arrive every month or so, sometimes every week. They can't cope with those boys. Breaking things is their idea of fun; they're a five-man wrecking crew. After all that's happened to them you'd think they would be subdued, but they're wilder than ever."

"That's why we're relying on you, Gloria. You're not only giving them emotional support but also the continuity they desperately need."

"The Nyebergers," she replied with feeling, "desperately need to be locked in a cage. Only yesterday the twins got my brand-new coat out of the hall closet and stuffed it down the toilet, blocking the system. A plumber had to come in and take the whole thing apart. Flub claimed they'd been trying to wash off some paint they'd poured on the coat. When I questioned them they admitted to stealing the paint from a neighbor's garage; they'll steal anything that's not nailed down. 'We thought you'd look better in red,' he told me, 'but then we didn't like it very much.' My coat's ruined, of course."

"Flub?"

"Philip. They're called Flub and Dub."

"Well, there you are!" Congreve exulted. "You've become so engaged with them you use their nicknames."

"Only because they won't answer to anything else. In fact they won't answer to much of anything, Chief. I know the only alternative to the current arrangement is to put them in a private facility and the Staunton lawyers are against it, but—"

"They're more than against it, Gloria. If we recommend to the court that the boys be institutionalized, the lawyers will cut off the generous annual grant this hospital receives from the family trust. We can't afford to lose that much money. Surely you can appreciate the position we're in."

As she walked down the echoing marble hall of the hospital Gloria Delmonico was a troubled woman. She and Gerry had considered themselves moderately well off until the Change disrupted lives and ruined economies. Now they had the two children they had wanted for so long and feared they might never have, but Gerry was no longer employed at Rob-Benn. No one in this part of the state was hiring industrial chemists. The River Valley Transportation Service was barely breaking even.

Gloria's salary at the hospital was vital.

"Surely you can appreciate the position *I'm* in," she whispered under her breath. Tomorrow she should say it out loud to Mitch Congreve. But she knew she wouldn't.

She also knew how Gerry would react if she said she wanted to quit the hospital. He would smile that big smile of his and say, "Whatever you want, Muffin. We'll get by."

They wouldn't get by.

They wouldn't even be able to keep up the mortgage.

Gloria looked at her watch, the little diamond-studded watch Gerry had given her on their third anniversary. *Count only the happy hours* was engraved on the back. Would the watch provide enough money for a house payment? Or two, maybe?

She sighed. Talking with Mitch Congreve had made her late for the horse-bus. It wouldn't call at the hospital again for another hour.

The nursery supplied for the children of hospital staff was in an annex behind the main building, with a babysitter in full-time attendance. When Gloria reached the back door she could hear the rain driving against it. Should she leave the kids in the nursery or bring them into the hospital? There was no decision to make; she wanted them with her. But she would need an umbrella.

A large brass jardinière beside the door held a supply of umbrellas kept for such occasions. One had a silvery goose head for a handle. She lifted it from the jardinière, leaned her shoulder against the door and pushed hard while opening the umbrella.

The ribs sprang wide. Collapsed. The silvery goose head morphed into something else.

By the time the premier carriage of the River Valley Transportation Service pulled up at the front entrance to the hospital the rain had stopped. Gerry Delmonico found his wife still sheltering under the portico. A small girl was holding one of her hands and a baby in a pale blue sleeper was cradled in her other arm. Gloria being late for the horse-bus wasn't unusual; emergencies took precedence over schedules, and emergencies requiring the services of a psychologist were more frequent since the Change.

The expression on Gloria's face was far from usual.

With a hasty command to the team to stand still, Gerry jumped from the driver's seat and hurried to his wife. "What's wrong, Muffin?"

"Here, hold the baby while I get something out of my backpack." The something proved to be one of her handkerchiefs, knotted around a handful of pale sand. "This was the top of an umbrella handle an hour ago, in the shape of a goose head. When I tried to open it the . . . well, the whole thing came apart. Take us home, will you? And toss this thing in the weeds along the way. I only kept it to show you."

———

Maybelline and Erasmus Barber were settling down after supper when someone rang their doorbell. Maybelline was frowning over a book of crossword puzzles; Barber was lighting his pipe. "Leave it," he instructed his wife.

"We can't do that, it might be important."

"Everything's important to some dam' fool," he growled. After the third ring of the bell, his reluctant feet dragged him to the door.

"Sorry, Gerry," Barber apologized, "but I've been pestered so much lately. This about your friend's car again?"

"It's closer to home. My wife tried to open an umbrella and the silver handle came apart in her hand. Sort of like the Mustang, only different," Gerry Delmonico added lamely. "My wife wanted me to throw it away but I thought you'd better see it first."

"Uh-huh. You bring it with you?"

Gerry removed the knotted handkerchief from a pocket in his jacket. "Here, have a look. What would make silver do this? Gloria's afraid the Change is coming back."

Barber carried the handkerchief to the nearest strong lamp and untied the knots. After studying it for a moment he said, "In the first place this wasn't silver, Gerry. It's nickel alloyed with copper and zinc, then polished to look like silver. It's called nickel silver, they use it in costume jewelry

91

and tableware. Even sterling silver contains alloys; so does the gold in your wedding ring. Pure metal's simply too soft to hold a shape on its own. Interesting thing about nickel, though. I took a sample from Jack Reece's car and when I put it through the X-ray I discovered nickel was the missing alloy."

"I'm not surprised," said Gerry. "When I worked at Rob-Benn I used nickel-lined containers for concentrated solutions of sodium hydroxide because nickel's highly resistant to alkali. That would make it a useful component in automotive steel too. But the Change only affected plastics and not—"

"And not metal," Barber interrupted. "You can reassure your wife on that score."

Gerry was not satisfied. "Is there some connection between plastics and metal that would make them both vulnerable to the same mechanism?"

"You think the Change was a 'mechanism' of some sort?"

"Only if you subscribe to the belief that everything in nature can be explained by physics or chemistry. I do, but it's one of the topics we've debated a lot at the Wednesday Club. Jack Reece takes the opposing view. He puts a certain amount of faith in intangibles, which is surprising, considering his background."

"How so?"

"He's sort of a jack-of-all-trades; among other things he's done work for the petrochemical industry. Industrial espionage, maybe; one can never be quite sure about Jack. During the Change he explained to us why different plastic objects were failing at different times. No matter what the finished item looks like, all plastics are composed of long chains of polymers that are easily manipulated. They react according to size and polymer construction; it takes some longer than others. Some might not be visibly affected within a person's lifetime, which is why the Change appeared so random. But plastic doesn't break down. Even when it looks like it's melting it's actually dissolving into tiny particles that could last hundreds of years. That's what makes the damned stuff such a plague on the planet."

While Gerry spoke Barber had been stirring the little pile of sand with his forefinger. His cheeks were sucked in; his eyes were troubled. "Metal's totally different," he said. "Forging metal is constructive, decomposing plastic is destructive. On a microscopic level all metals are crystalline solids with closely packed atoms. They rely on their relationship to one another for form. That's a basic law of physics; there are no exceptions. The nickel alloy in your friend's car failed *structurally*, which is what caused the steel to collapse. I would have said such a thing is metalurgically impossible. And so is this . . . this umbrella handle, or whatever it was. Perhaps it's another example of random destruction. By whom? And for what purpose?" He looked up. "We're beginning to wade in deep waters, my friend."

# 7

"So here you are at last, Jack," Edgar Tilbury said when he opened his front door on a cloudy Sunday morning. "I wondered when you'd come."

"Curiosity is a powerful itch."

"I'm guessing it was more than that. The explosion in the Baltic, maybe?"

"That was part of it."

Tilbury's piercing gaze shifted to the woman partially concealed behind Jack. "I'm glad to see you brought someone with you. Don't be shy, Nell, the invitation was meant for you too; for anyone who's close to Jack. Within reason, of course; this isn't Noah's Ark."

Nell said, "I have two kids and my mother."

"And I have Aunt Bea," Jack added. "But you know that already."

"Of course Bea's included, I planned to invite her myself." Tilbury's tangled eyebrows collided in a frown. "I believe she has a cat, Jack?"

"Cats in the plural. You might need to rethink that remark about Noah's Ark. All her cats are neutered, though."

"That's not the problem. I have a cat allergy."

"Nobody's perfect," Jack said cheerfully. "You've heard the old song: 'You can't have one without the other.' That's my aunt and her cats. You might want to stock up on allergy medication if you're serious about having her."

"The kids and I have two Irish setters, Edgar," Nell interjected. "Biggish ones."

"That's okay, dogs don't bother me. There's plenty of room down there and we can lay in crates of dog food."

Jack said, "I hate to keep spoiling the party, but I didn't grow up in Bea Fontaine's house without learning a lot about cats. Dogs can live on cat food but cats won't thrive on dog food; it doesn't contain the enzyme cats need for their eyesight."

"I try to learn something new every day," Tilbury responded. "We'll get both kinds, along with a big supply of horse feed. I've already promised Shay Mulligan that Evan can put his mare and her two-year-old colt in the barn. They'll be almost as safe as we are; the underside of the roof is lined with lead to protect the animals in here."

"Are you ready for all this?" Nell asked. "It seems like a lot to take on."

"Don't worry about me, but thanks for your concern. You have a considerate woman here, Jack."

"She has a lot of virtues," Jack agreed. Raising one eyebrow, he added, "And just enough vices to be interesting. We're planning to get married soon, so I wanted her to know about this if—"

"If it's an option in her future. You'd better look at the arrangements, then. Follow me out to the barn."

Nell said doubtfully, "A barn doesn't sound like much of a bomb shelter, Edgar, even with a lead roof."

"Wait and see."

Tilbury led them to a large barn perched on a hill at the rear of his property. The barn was newer than his white frame farmhouse and had been constructed in a different style. Seen close up it hardly looked like a barn, more like a factory with timber siding.

Instead of sliding open the heavy wooden doors at the front, Edgar took the couple around to the south side and opened a small access door.

There was a sudden scurrying and flapping of wings.

Nell laughed. "How did those chickens get in?"

"They have the equivalent of a cat flap," said Tilbury.

"And they're smart enough to use it?"

"Chickens are a lot smarter than people think. They don't like the rain so they spend most of their time in here. That big rooster is a Rhode Island Red; fertilized eggs are better for you. The hens are his harem."

"Lucky guy," said Jack.

The air inside the barn smelled of hay and feathers.

Much of the floor space was occupied by farm equipment, stacked bales of hay and straw and several empty horse stalls. There were also a few horse-drawn vehicles: a pony cart, an elegantly shaped brougham with a driver's seat in front, and a partially completed surrey waiting for the fringe on top. Nell gravitated to them immediately. "You built these yourself, Edgar?" Before he could reply she answered her own question. "Of course you did; you made the carriage for the horse-bus."

He was pleased that she recognized his handiwork. "It's an unusual hobby, I suppose, but my late wife and I spent the first days of our honeymoon in New York. Then we cut the trip short. The city was too big and too loud and Mary Veronica was a very shy girl. Her parents had christened her Mary Veronica, I loved the name, but she thought it was ostentatious. That will tell you something about her. She said that New York made her want to crawl into a hole and pull it in after her. People had that effect on her. I have a reputation for being a hermit; she was the real thing.

"Veronica never forgot driving through Central Park in a carriage; she talked about it for the rest of her life. She loved what she called 'old timey things'; we had that in common. I decided that someday we would go back there. Not to see the city, just to drive through the park one more time. But you know how it is, things get pushed ahead to the future because you're sure there will be a future. In the meantime I was building up my business and she was dreaming about the family we would have. She said she wanted to raise them in the country because her grandparents had been country people.

"Then she got sick and Central Park disappeared under a foot of water when the sea rose. What you plan for is rarely what happens.

"I bought a farm as my way of taking her back to the land. We remodeled the old farmhouse and filled it with the things we loved, but fresh air couldn't save her. Neither could the best doctors. That's when I learned what money's really worth. Nada, zilch, zero." His voice had gone cold. "Money's made from dead trees, so what would you expect?

"Before Veronica died she made me promise I would go on living for her sake. Hardest promise I ever made, but she loved life, so I tried. I began building the reproduction carriages as a tribute to her. Then I realized I needed a bigger project." He paused, looking inward. "Something to defy death, the enemy I hadn't been able to defeat."

Jack and Nell exchanged glances.

Tilbury said, "What I'm going to show you was adapted from German plans drawn up during World War One. They engineered a sophisticated system of tunnels underground beneath No Man's Land. The Germans provided their troops with light, sanitation, even kitchens and libraries; they were more comfortable than the Allied generals on the surface. Makes you wonder how they could have lost, doesn't it?

"The blueprints for the tunnels were discovered after the war; some went into museums or private collections. Many years later I saw a set of drawings at an auction and bought them as an engineering curiosity. I threw them into a drawer when I got home and forgot about them for a while. When I finally got around to examining them I saw a possible way to defy death, mine or someone else's. Not forever, you understand, but for a while.

"By that time I'd sold my business; without Veronica, what was I working so hard for? But I had no trouble getting the help and equipment I needed. My former connections were still good, and workmen will do anything if you pay them well enough. I started to dig my first tunnel where this barn is now. It took a lot of manpower and machinery. Folks around here mostly leave their neighbors alone, but when they asked what I was doing I said I needed more space for my hobby. Crackpot Tilbury, they called me. Gone loopy in his old age."

He chuckled. "Eventually they had to concede I was a smart businessman. During the Change when motorized transport got scarce I had more customers coming here for my carriages and pony carts than I could handle."

"But why the barn?" Jack asked.

Nell's face lit up. "Because it's the perfect camouflage for a fortress."

"Good girl!" said Tilbury. "I didn't want anything to be obvious. During the scare about nuclear war in the last century people were afraid their neighbors would kill them to get access to their shelters. There were some pretty nasty incidents; juries didn't always accept the excuse of 'self-defense.' I don't believe there's any more reason to trust my fellow man in this century, so I keep quiet about what I have.

"There's a warren of man-made tunnels and natural lime-stone caves down there. Once you go underground the temperature doesn't vary more than a few degrees, it always feels like an autumn day. I've installed an industrial generator and a backup system to be sure of plenty of light and power, and a hotel water heater—"

"Can I recharge my car from your generator?"

"If you have the attachment, but you'll need a pretty long cable."

"What about fuel for the generator?"

"Two years' worth of diesel, and before you ask, it's vented to the outside. Any longer than two years . . ." Edgar hesitated. "Any longer and survival may not be worth it."

"I prefer to make that decision for myself," Jack said crisply. "I don't quit before the fight starts. Go on; what other machines do you have?"

"Electric fans to circulate the air; I expect it could get pretty stale. And a heavy-duty dehumidifier. It won't dry out the air underground but it should protect my library."

"If your books were micro-engraved on glass discs," Jack pointed out, "you wouldn't need a dehumidifier."

"No, and I wouldn't read much either; it would take too much time to convert the tiny little lines on the discs back to text. That's how we're going to lose more libraries than the burning of Alexandria. The water my dehumidifier collects is stored for washing and should be safe enough to drink if necessary; it's been filtered through limestone. I'm going to take more bottled water down there anyway before—"

"'Before,'" said Jack. Tasting the word. "How long do you think we have *before?*"

"Lila has access to the facilities at the newspaper, both the international wire services and the shortwave. She monitors them frequently and she'll let me know . . . let me know when. Most of her stuff is already down there, same as mine."

"How does she contact you?"

Tilbury smiled thinly. "There are only two professions for a thinking man: law and engineering. I don't have a hell of a lot of respect for the law but I fully appreciate the benefits of engineering, and I'm a first-rate tinkerer. You've got your Japanese AllCom, Jack; I've cobbled together my own version, which is almost as good. Lila has one and I have another. I even made some for friends."

"I have an old AllCom that belonged to my late husband," Nell interjected. "It's one of those that still works."

"Good to know," said Tilbury. He used a barn broom to brush aside loose straw, revealing a heavy trapdoor set flush with the floor. Two bicycles were propped against the nearest wall. "Pedal power," he explained, "for emergencies."

"You must expect a lot of emergencies."

"It's the principle of the inverse ratio, Jack. The better you're prepared for emergencies, the fewer you have." He glanced down at Nell's feet. "Those shoes you're wearing were meant for city streets; I suggest you take them off."

"Are we going below?"

"We are. I'll go first, Jack can bring up the rear."

"Then I'll keep my shoes on, thank you."

Tilbury shrugged. "Have it your way. At first there was only an inclined passage going down, but if I fell and broke something I figured I could lie there a mighty long time before anybody found me. There are wooden steps in the shaft now, just be sure you hold on to that rope at the side."

Nell gave Jack a look that said accusingly, *he's your friend!* She took a deep breath and followed Tilbury down the stairs. Jack followed close behind. "Is it hard to open that trapdoor from below, Edgar?"

"Just put your shoulder to it."

"I mean, suppose a woman or a child needed to get out?"

"No problem."

Jack was not reassured.

Halfway down the stairs he could feel a change in the temperature.

Nell could smell the embracing earth.

Down and down.

She trailed her fingertips along the wall and felt a slight dampness.

"Edgar? Does it ever flood down here?"

"There's a certain amount of seepage but that's to be expected with limestone. I've installed pumps in the low places, and both of the exterior doors are watertight in case of flooding aboveground."

"Both?"

"Nell, you should never have just one way of getting in and out. Another name for that sort of arrangement is 'dead end.' Prairie dogs, ground squirrels, badgers . . . many sentient creatures that live underground give themselves a back door. That even includes spiders."

"I never thought of spiders as being sentient."

"How can we judge what's 'sentient' and what isn't? I looked that word up once. It means 'able to perceive or feel things.' Even trees may be . . . watch out now, you're getting to the bottom."

Darkness waited at the foot of the steps. Tilbury flicked a switch, flooding the area with light. On a shelf nearby stood a row of flashlights. "LEDs," he said, "to carry with you if you need them going up or down."

"You have plenty of batteries?"

"Of course, Jack; boxes of them. There's a lot of things down here that run on batteries."

"Batteries are metal for the most part," Jack commented. "Have you examined yours recently?"

"They're okay," said Tilbury. "I wouldn't overlook anything like that."

The shaft opened into an L-shaped gallery. Three tunnels branched off from this space, each lined with wooden shelves laden with provisions. Clearly labeled boxes and cartons and cans and jars were arranged in order as far as the light revealed. Beneath them on the cement floor was a forest of large glass bottles filled with water.

Nell looked up at the low ceiling. "That's not going to collapse on us, is it?"

"The walls and ceiling are supported with timbers made from railway sleepers and they're lined with layers of reinforced concrete. Doing that was the hardest part of the job. The guys working for me complained about it, said I didn't need to go to all that trouble. But when you're writing the paycheck you can have your own way."

"You've thought of everything."

"Probably not, Nell; I'm good but not that good. There's bound to be something important that I forgot, so I've filled a cavern with building supplies we might need in the future."

"This isn't a bomb shelter, it's more like a shopping mall. My daughter will love it."

"Or hate it," said Jack.

# 8

When the pebbles struck her bedroom window Jessamyn Bennett laughed. Standing behind a curtain so he could not see her face, she reached around to open the sash and called to the young man on the lawn below, "That is so *oldcom,* Evan! D'you think you're Romano or somebody?"

"Romeo. And no, I don't, I just wanted to see you."

"We have a perfectly good front door, you know."

"If I knocked on it the dogs would bark. This way I thought you'd come down and let me in without disturbing them. Or your mother."

"Why'd you think I'd let you in at all?"

"Aw, Jess, don't be like that. That fight we had yesterday . . ."

"Was stupid, but you were wrong. I hate the idea of your being a soldier."

"Someone has to defend the country."

"I thought you were going to be a vet like your father."

"If there's a war . . . hey, we can't keep shouting like this, your mother . . ."

"She's gone off somewhere with Jack Reece."

"On Sunday morning? They go to church?"

"You must be kidding."

"Well, if she's not here, why can't you let me in?"

She considered the heated curlers in her hair and the depilatory cream on her upper lip. Glanced at her still unmade bed. "Wait just a minute," she called down.

Almost ten minutes passed before she opened one of the front doors.

Sunday was Gloria Delmonico's favorite day. She loved going to church with her husband and two small children. Like their parents before them, they were members of St. Anne's on the corner of Pine Grove and Alcott Place. Gloria and Gerry had met in Sunday school there. Childhood sweethearts, they had been together ever since.

The steeple of the old church was like a finger pointing to God. Thick stone walls imparted a cushioned serenity to the atmosphere inside, enhanced by the lemony scent of furniture polish on the pews and the fragrance of the flower arrangements, which were changed every week by the ladies of the parish.

On a sunny day, radiant light filtered through the stained glass windows on either side of the central aisle. Gloria's favorite depicted the Good Shepherd with his flock in a verdant pasture. Man and beast were fresh from the Creator's hand, their beauty more apparent than their differences. The windows had been assembled by artisans who knew their trade. Each piece of glass was precisely cut and snugly fitted into a secure lead frame. For over two centuries those windows had resisted storm and hail, birds blundering against them and an occasional ball flung by naughty boys.

At the last census Gloria had described herself to the census taker as "a sometime churchgoer," but that claim was dictated by her need to be honest. Her church attendance depended on whether she was on duty at the hospital. If not, the Delmonico family occupied the third pew on the Gospel side, close to the serene Shepherd and his flock. The troubles of the outside world could not touch them there.

This morning Gloria looked around surreptitiously, wondering how many of her fellow parishioners were thinking about God. Some probably were worrying about their jobs, or their unpaid bills, or comparing the clothes they were wearing with what someone else wore. She knew that because she did it herself, then felt guilty.

Gerry had gone outside with their infant son, who was fretful again. In church they took turns with that chore. Their small daughter leaned against her mother's knees and scribbled in one of the hymnals. When Gloria tried to rescue the book she protested, "I wighting songs!"

Maybe you are, her mother thought. And maybe I'm stifling your creative impulses.

While she was mentally weighing right and wrong, debating whether to surrender or discipline, a large object slammed against the outside of the stained glass window. Serenity shuddered from the impact, held for a second longer . . . then collapsed into the church in a rainbow shower of glass.

The damaged Good Shepherd lay amid his broken sheep.

Gloria clutched her daughter to her chest, jumped to her feet and fled the pew.

A heartbeat later Gerry raced into the church with their infant son in his arms. He thundered up the aisle, shouldering other people aside and shouting his wife's name.

"We're all right!" she called.

A crowd was gathering around the invader lying on the floor below the ruined window. Although roughly the size and shape of a coffin lid, the edges were ragged, as if they had been ripped away. "That looks like the door off an airplane," someone said.

"But how did it—"

The question was interrupted by a terrific explosion.

As one person, the congregation abandoned the church and rushed outside to stare at the column of black smoke rising from the center of town.

Lila Ragland was the first reporter on the scene through a lucky accident—lucky for her but not for many. After a late night with Shay Mulligan she awoke with a ferocious headache she didn't want to admit. When he finally kissed her good-bye she set out for the Corner Pharmacy for aspirin. The drugstore was only a few blocks from her one-bedroom apartment on Cleveland Street, just off Elm, the main street bisecting town and running from northwest to southeast. The convenient location was one of the reasons Lila had taken the apartment. The offices of *The Sycamore Seed* were also within walking distance, though in the opposite direction.

Since the end of the Change, aircraft were beginning to fly again. Lila glanced up to see one passing overhead. The autumn day was unusually sunny; she could feel the plane's cool shadow on her face. That's much too low, she thought. Then she realized the aircraft wasn't flying but *falling;* falling out of the sky as a leaf might.

Other objects were falling with it.

Lila ducked into the shelter of the nearest doorway, the portico of the public library. From this vantage point she saw a hail of objects strike the ground; everything from unidentifiable slabs of metal to intact luggage. Some ricocheted; a sharp-edged metallic triangle barely missed spearing through her leg. The aircraft was leaving a debris field to mark the path of its disintegration. But no body parts, her shocked yet still observing mind reported. So there was no midair explosion . . .

The explosion came soon enough. It shook the earth as the doomed plane plowed into the center of the town.

Within minutes a blackened marble shell was all that remained of the defunct Sycamore and Staunton Mercantile Bank.

Goettinger's Department Store, Deel's Hardware, The

Magic Carpet, Ye Olde Booke Wurm, Gold's Court Florist, the Corner Pharmacy (Open Till Ten), the Fletcher Building, Ralph Williams' Insurance Agency, Snips Hairdressers, In-a-Minnit Dry Cleaners—and Bill's Bar and Grill had ceased to exist.

# 9

After their tour of what Tilbury persisted in calling "my bolt-hole," he took Jack and Nell back to his house for a drink. "You'll need one after that," he assured them.

"We must have walked miles."

"Not quite, Nell, but there was a lot of up and down. You'll feel it in your legs and your back tomorrow."

She gave him a rueful smile. "I feel it now."

The rambling frame building that appeared to be a simple farmhouse from the outside was different inside. Deep pockets and Veronica Tilbury's taste had combined to produce sophisticated rusticity. The living room was papered in a muted blue-and-white stripe; the huge brick fireplace could have held a roasting ox. From the raftered, white-painted ceiling hung an elegant bronze-and-crystal chandelier. Empty bookshelves gave mute testimony to a large personal library, recently relocated. A well-worn recliner upholstered in coppery velour waited beside a large floor lamp, anticipating a similar move soon. In the center of the room was a square French provincial coffee table with two chairs on either side.

Tilbury served his guests their drinks in Waterford crystal tumblers wrapped in paper napkins. "It's still Sunday morning but a man's home is his castle and this is mine, so I declare a special dispensation."

Nell sniffed the contents of her glass. "Whiskey?"

"Jameson, that's all we drink around here."

"Jack told me there was an artesian well on the property."

He rolled an eye at her. "You want to put water in good whiskey?"

She took a tiny sip. Rewarded him with a bright smile. "No way; I'll drink mine neat from now on."

Even with most of its furnishings missing, the room looked comfortable. I wonder how much of that's down to Veronica, Nell asked herself. Spirit of place . . .

"Penny for your thoughts," said Jack.

She gazed into her glass. "While we were down there, I kept thinking about the Cathari."

"The what?"

"Not what; who." She took another drink of her whiskey.

"Cathari," Tilbury echoed. "Now where did I read about them?"

Nell turned toward him. "Archaeology's an enthusiasm of mine, Edgar. When I was a child there was a program on public broadcasting about the discovery of a 'lost city,' and that's what started my interest in old ruins. An archaeologist had uncovered the remains of a great hilltop fortress in France, built in the twelfth century by a large Christian sect called the Cathari. The Cathari believed in dualism, the theory of two opposed principles at work in the universe, like the Chinese yin and yang. They held that the spiritual world was good and the material world was evil. Humans were corrupted and—"

"In today's world it's hard to argue with that premise," Jack said.

Ignoring him, she went on. "The Cathari believed their purpose in life was to free their spirits from material chains and restore their communion with God. They developed an organized religion with a complete system of doctrine, a hierarchy and a liturgy. They even reinterpreted the Bible; rather drastically, it seems. Their followers spread through France and Italy, preaching an extreme form of asceticism that divided them into two groups, the 'Perfect,' who renounced all the temptations of the flesh, and the 'Believers,' who weren't expected to live up to their standards but did their best."

"The 'Perfect' wouldn't give up sex, eh? Put me down for the other crowd."

"Please, Jack, I'm trying to explain something! Because the Cathari doctrines struck at the roots of the Christian establishment and its political institutions they were labeled as heretics. This was the era of the Crusades; on the pretext of driving out unbelievers, armies led by Christian knights and barons went rampaging from Europe across the Middle East. Most of them were more interested in plunder than in religion, and they enjoyed hunting down so-called heretics and putting them to the sword. Or torturing them to death; this was the time of the Inquisition too.

"The stronghold of the Perfect was a self-contained community near the Pyrenees, the ruined fortress that fascinated me as a child. You'll understand why I was reminded of it today. The inhabitants had everything they needed there, so they could spend their time in prayer and meditation. Because they kept to themselves to avoid earthly temptations, the Crusaders assumed the Cathari must have a fortune hidden somewhere on the mountain."

"What happened to them?" Jack was suddenly serious.

"An army marched to the Cathari fortress and began slaughtering the peasants who lived in the foothills."

"I remember!" cried Tilbury. "It's in the *Encyclopedia Britannica;* the real one, not the Fake-ipedia. The Albigensian Crusade, wasn't that what it was called?"

Nell was pleased that they shared this snippet of esoteric knowledge. "The Crusaders built a huge fire at the base of the mountain and taunted the Cathari. They dared them to come down, if they were so holy, and save the local people from further torture. But it was a trap. The Crusaders intended to seize the heretics when they left their stronghold, tie them to stakes and burn them alive.

"The stakes weren't necessary.

"When the fire was at its height, the Perfect came down the mountain singing and gave themselves to the flames."

# 10

There was a long silence in the room. Silence as soft as ancient ashes.

"Perfect timing," Jack said at last. "Either of you hear that?"

"Hear what?"

He set his glass down on the table. "Sirens."

Nell was annoyed with him for breaking the spell. "You're teasing."

After a moment Tilbury said, "I hear them too. Sounds like the Benning Volunteer Brigade. But unless I'm wrong they're headed away from town, toward Sycamore River."

"Sycamore River has its own fire department."

Tilbury put down his glass and stood up. "Then they must need help; let's go see what's happening."

Jack's coupé had been designed for two passengers or three very close friends. Only after he had taken delivery did he realize the car excluded the rest of Nell's family. She hadn't mentioned it. Not yet. And he was not ready to trade it in on a larger model.

Not yet.

As they stood on the front porch of Tilbury's house there

was a hasty conference. "You can sit on my lap," Tilbury told Nell, "if you don't mind bony knees."

"Can't you drive your pickup?"

"I could, but whatever's happened would be over before it got there."

"Then I accept your offer," Nell said with a smile.

When they reached the highway that linked the two towns Tilbury asked, "Is that radio working?"

"I haven't tried it yet; wait a sec." Keeping an eye on the road—though it wasn't necessary, the car was preprogrammed to go to Bill's Bar and Grill—Jack pressed a button on the control panel. A New York accent said, ". . . casting service, with an important announcement from the civil def—" and was abruptly interrupted by the hiss and crackle of static.

"Damn!" Jack pushed the button harder. The static rose in volume. Filled the interior of the car like a storm of sleet against the window glass.

Nell leaned forward, waiting impatiently for clear air.

When the static faded the suave voice assured listeners, "This notice will be repeated on the quarter hour, so stay tuned. In the meantime we return to the latest release from The Dead Fucks, their chart-topping 'You Piss Me Off.'"

"You piss me off," Nell said angrily. "Doesn't anyone play real music anymore?"

"I've got a good selection down below," Tilbury told her. "Country and western, popular, classical—you prefer Chopin or Mahler?"

"Jazz," Jack interjected. "Three-in-the-morning cool jazz."

From the highway they could see smoke rising in the direction of Sycamore River. "Black smoke," Tilbury announced, squinting. "Like airplane fuel; there must've been a crash."

The highway and access roads going into town were beginning to receive traffic. No one was coming in the other direction. Jack started to override the preset destination, then thought better of it. He instructed the VC to go faster. "You already have reached the legal speed limit for a passenger vehicle," the sexy voice informed him.

"Then break the damned limit!" Jack shouted at the control panel.

"That is not possible," was the polite reply. "Predetermined speeds are a major safety feature of our highways."

Tilbury peered around Nell's shoulder. "Looks like the smoke's coming from the center of town."

"It's nowhere near your house," Jack assured Nell. "Your kids are at home, aren't they?"

"I think Jess is, but Colin mentioned working at Deel's this morning. Or maybe he said next week, I wasn't really listening."

"Deel's is open on Sunday?"

"Who observes Sunday anymore?" Nell asked.


The staff of the Hilda Staunton Memorial Hospital did not observe Sunday. Some nonessential personnel like Gloria

Delmonico had the day off, but the emergency department was fully staffed—as always, following Saturday night.

For years the board of directors had endured complaints about the location of the hospital. When it was originally envisioned by the Staunton family, the matriarch of the clan had insisted it be built adjacent to the residential area on the south side of the river. "That's where our patients will come from," Hilda had said—ignoring the fact that people on the less-affluent north side would get sick too.

Hilda's lack of a social conscience meant the hospital was not in the pathway of the doomed aircraft. Within fifteen minutes the first casualties began to arrive. Every member of the staff was summoned to report at once.


Colin Bennett had been given the keys to the hardware store and a list of jobs that needed doing while the business was closed. Cleaning toilets was demeaning—surely the army never asked officers to do that—but painting woodwork and cleaning a skylight were within Colin's ambit.

He preferred to do the hardest thing first, so he had scrubbed the bathroom before moving on to the painting. Colin was slow but thorough; it was nearing noon when he opened the tallest ladder in the store and climbed up to have a look at the skylight. The glass was coated with grime on the outside, preventing any contribution to the light within the store. To make matters worse the metal frame was warped and the mechanism that opened it was jammed. Colin had a screwdriver in his back pocket but it wasn't sufficient for the task; he would have to go onto the flat roof.

First he took a candy bar from his pocket and sat down in a wheelbarrow to eat it. Slowly, savoring every bite, licking the melted chocolate from his fingers afterward. After wadding up the candy wrapper and looking unsuccessfully for a container to put it in, he stuffed the paper into the back pocket of his jeans along with his wallet, folded the ladder and carried it around to the rear of the building. Colin was almost six feet tall, but the ladder was awkward to handle. No wonder these things aren't selling, he said to himself. And we definitely need to order more trash cans, I'll tell the boss in the morning.

When the ladder was securely in place he climbed to the roof. The gutter was stuffed with leaves.

Do the job now and tell him tomorrow, that'll show initiative.

Colin stepped out onto the roof and looked around.

The block where Deel's Hardware stood was on a slight rise he had never noticed from the street. He took a moment to enjoy the view. Row after row of rooftops were gift-wrapped by the curve of the river, a shimmering blue ribbon that reflected the sky.

Nice phrase, he told himself. Maybe I could be a writer?

Colin Bennett never saw the huge lump of metal that plummeted down upon him.

---

Fuel from the explosion burned fiercely in the center of town. Pieces of the airplane and miscellaneous debris littered the area for blocks, together with the broken bodies of passengers and crew. A few who had survived the impact staggered about, dazed, looking for help. Or for anyone who could tell them who they were.

Because it was Sunday morning a number of lives were saved. The former bank building stood vacant, a white elephant the real estate agent had yet to sell. Goettinger's Department Store, the travel agency and the bookshop were closed. They were destroyed but provided no human victims.

Martha Frobisher, who owned Gold's Court Florist, had gone to the shop to check on the arrangements for a funeral the following morning. Martha was a widow herself; she wanted to be certain every detail was perfect for the deceased's wife and family. Part of the tail assembly of the plane broke through the roof of the florist shop and decapitated its conscientious owner.

The Corner Pharmacy had been busy as usual; Lila Ragland was not the only person who needed a headache remedy after Saturday night.

The two clerks on duty that Sunday morning were doing a brisk trade in aspirin and other analgesics. A few customers were looking for stronger pain relief, and a girl in her teens and a long-married woman both requested the morning-after pill. The man behind the counter had heard it all before. The only person he felt sorry for was the current housekeeper for the young Stauntons, who begged him to refill her prescription for Valium long before it was due.

He was about to comply when the nose of the aircraft burst through the front of the drugstore, killing eleven customers outright and maiming the pharmacist for life.

The offices in the Fletcher Building and Ralph Williams' Insurance Agency were closed, as were Snips Hairdressers and In-a-Minnit Dry Cleaners. But Bill's Bar and Grill was full on Sunday morning because Marla prepared a delicious brunch buffet, where Lacey Strawbridge and Bud Moriarty were among those who regularly enjoyed the best Bloody Marys in town. That Sunday they were bloody indeed. Bill's was ground zero for disaster.

Jessamyn Bennett and Evan Mulligan had spent an engrossing morning until Jess became aware of the time. She could not remember if Colin had said he would be home for lunch. "We'd better get dressed and go downstairs," she warned Evan. "It'd be just like my weasel brother to show up now and catch us."

"What if he does? You don't answer to him."

"That's not the point; you don't have a younger brother or you'd know. Colin would tell Mom all about our 'orgy,' and what he couldn't guess he'd make up. He's always trying to score points against me."

"And I suppose you don't do that to him?"

Jess had the grace to laugh.

Fully dressed, they were telling one another good-bye in the living room when the doorbell chimed. The dogs went wild. As the setters raced to the front door they were barking furiously.

"Sheila!" Jess shouted. "Rocky, you be quiet now!" When she opened the door she found two uniformed police officers waiting; one was a woman she knew. Her husband was important in local government and they lived only a couple of blocks away. When Colin was younger he had mowed their lawn every other Saturday. "Is your mother home, Jessamyn?" she asked.

"No, Mrs. Collier . . . I mean Officer . . . I don't know when she'll be back, but if you'd like me to give her a message . . ."

"Can we come in?"

Something was wrong; Jess felt saliva flood her mouth.

Officer Collier asked her to sit down before they talked, and joined her on the couch. Evan stood to one side uncertainly, watching the scene but not part of it. Not really wanting to be part of it. The male officer waited by the door with his hands behind his back, endeavoring to maintain a detached expression.

The female officer said, "I'm afraid we have some bad news. There's been an accident, Jessamyn. Your brother Colin—"

"That bicycle of his, he's always so careless. Is he—"

The male officer cleared his throat. "It wasn't a traffic accident, Miss Bennett. He was on the roof of Deel's Hardware when a large object fell on him."

"On the *roof*? That's crazy. What kind of object?"

"We don't know yet."

"How bad was he hurt?"

"Nothing could be done, I'm afraid," said the woman in a voice so low Jess could hardly make out the words. "His skull was crushed."

"Are you sure it's him?" Jess's lips had gone numb; it felt like someone else was asking the question.

"He had a wallet in his pocket with a driver's license and some credit cards in the name of Colin Bennett."

Jess sat frozen, waiting for the pain.

This wasn't happening. She had fallen asleep after they made love and this was a crazy nightmare.

They were all watching her.

She didn't know how to wake up.

"We require a formal identification by a family member," the male officer said, "but it doesn't have to be right now. Would you rather wait for your mother?"

# 11

Paige Prentiss was happy with her job as a veterinary nurse. She loved animals and enjoyed meeting their owners. One of the perks of her employment was getting to keep her dog with her during the day. Usually Samson lay quietly behind the front counter; people did not know he was there unless he stood up and came around the corner.

The big Rottweiler was a serious deterrent to would-be drug thieves.

"He used to be called Satan," Paige explained when visitors to the clinic were nervous of him. "He was Robert Bennett's guard dog and he had a reputation for being terribly vicious, but that was all propaganda. Now his name is Samson and he's my darling. He's really an old sweetheart when you get to know him. He's terrified of loud noises and he won't go out in the rain. Isn't that right, Monkey Face?" At this point in the story she would fondle his ears while the dog squirmed with pleasure.

Tall, sturdy and competent, Paige wore no makeup; her hair, the color of brown sugar, hung to the small of her back in a thick braid as it had done since her school days. She had several boyfriends, none of them serious. "They may be but

I'm not" was how she put it. She donated to the SPCA and Save the Whales, and was a fervent supporter of the Daggett's Woods Conservancy. When Shay discovered just how generous was her support for her favorite charities he had given her a commensurate raise in pay, which she applied to the purchase of a modest bungalow near the center of town.

She wrote to her mother in Milwaukee, "I know I should walk to work but the doc hates me being late, so I ride my bicycle. The house is fantastic, it just needs a little work. Like more closet space. If you come to visit me at Christmas Dad can do the carpentry. He will just adore my dog, but it will take time to make friends with him. Samson doesn't like men very much."

Samson was not the only animal who spent most days in the clinic. Shay Mulligan's black cat named Karma, a gift from Lila Ragland, liked to lie on the front desk with her paws neatly tucked under her chest. From this vantage point she could regard visitors with a hypnotic gaze through immense blue-green eyes.

Since the veterinarian had begun spending his weekends with Lila, Paige did not like to leave the cat alone for so long. On Saturday evening she bundled Karma into a basket and fastened it to her bicycle for the ride home. As usual, Samson trotted along behind.

Sunday found Paige wearing a bikini and stretched out on a blanket in her backyard, hoping to top up a fading tan before cold weather set in. She believed that a tan made her look slimmer, and a sunny morning had become a rare commodity. Samson lay at her feet, enjoying a doze. Karma was curled up in the kitchen window, soaking up vitamin D through her black fur.

In spite of her best intentions, Paige had too much energy to lie unmoving in the sun for very long. There was an unopened package of Oreo cookies in the kitchen . . .

As she started to get up Samson threw back his head and began to howl.

The primordial cry blended with the thunder of disaster. Paige froze. Samson kept howling.

"Shut up, will you! That sounded like an explosion!"

Galvanized into action, Paige ran into her front yard and looked down the street.

Samson was right at her heels.

"Bombs," Tilbury intoned like the voice of doom. "Those are bombs, and we're going in the wrong direction."

Nell cried, "Take me home fast, Jack! I have to see if my children are all right."

"I'm going as fast as I can. As long as we're on the highway we—"

"Then turn off! Just beyond McCaffrey's gas station, turn left and go up Daggett's Lane toward the woods. Hurry!"

As Jack followed her instructions Tilbury mused aloud, "December seventh, 1941, the day that would live in infamy.

Pearl Harbor was a surprise attack like this. Why do we never learn? We're fond of predicting the future, but we never realize the future's arrived until it's too late. You two should be glad you're with me."

"But we're not in your bomb shelter," Jack pointed out, "and neither are Nell's kids or my Aunt Bea or anyone we care about. Disaster's always a surprise, Edgar, otherwise we'd act in time to prevent it."

"I thought I had." Tilbury twisted his body, trying to get a better view out the window. "Do either of you see any airplanes flying?"

"No."

"That's good. If this was a surprise bombing attack there'd be a squadron up there, or at least a bomber and a couple of fighters."

Jack said, "As soon as Nell checks on her children we'll drive into town and find out what happened."

"Whatever it was," Tilbury replied glumly, keeping his eyes fixed on the dark smoke, "we'll be too late to do much good."

As they pulled up to Nell's house she saw the police car parked in front, and went cold all over. "No. No no no . . ."

"Don't bleed till you're shot," Tilbury advised. Jack helped her out of the car. Jessamyn came running from the house and flung herself into her mother's arms. "It's Colin!" she wailed.

In one of the ironies that often accompany a disaster, those who observed the Christian Sabbath in Sycamore River had a lucky escape. Aside from the demolished window at St. Anne's, none of the churches holding services that day was damaged by the crash. Neither was the Jewish synagogue nor the town's only mosque.

Others not so fortunate found themselves in the wrong place at the wrong time. Victims were thronging into Staunton Memorial Hospital. Some arrived on improvised stretchers or were carried on blankets or in arms. Others walked, staggered, stumbled. Trails of blood streaked the parking lot. Ambulances wailed outside the Emergency entrance while frantic friends and relatives wailed inside, pleading for miracles.

Gerry Delmonico had taken their children home while Gloria, shaken but resolute, reported to Mitchell Congreve. "Thank God you're here!" he cried when he saw her hurrying down the hall toward him. "Some of our staff are unaccounted for, I only hope they're on their way and not . . . get into your scrubs as fast as you can, then go to the A and E. It's going to be a helluva day."

It was.

One of the victims Gloria could not help was found lying on the cement pavement outside the Emergency entrance, wearing only a bikini on her broken body. An unidentified Good Samaritan had found her and brought her there; she was unmistakably dead. The huge black dog beside her would not let anyone come close. When they tried, he raised his hackles and displayed a daunting set of fangs.

An intern shouted, "Somebody get this fuckin' beast outta the way!"

The dog was badly injured; a mangled front leg was almost severed from his body. His blood had drenched both of them but was beginning to clot.

Gloria's heart contracted with pity.

She bent her knees to make herself appear smaller and approached warily, careful not to meet his eyes. "Is she your person?" Gloria asked in a soft voice. "I won't hurt her. I won't hurt either of you, but I'd like to help if I can."

He whined.

She slowly extended a hand. "Please let me help."

The lifted hackles sank back by a fraction of an inch. The dog whined again; a beseeching voice at the center of chaos.

Long expected and feared, at first the catastrophe was assumed to be the opening stage in an international conflict. The Federal Aviation Administration and the local civil defense team were notified immediately. Both promised to send investigators at once and were able to assure people that war had not broken out.

"Not yet," the chairman of the FAA privately amended to his assistant. "Sounds like we've got a dry run, though."

The examination of the largest crash area began while bodies were still being removed. Men in protective boiler suits were poring through wreckage when Lila Ragland arrived, notebook and journalistic credentials in hand. "I'm sorry, miss," one of the men told her, "but no press allowed."

"Quite right too," she said. "This is a sensitive scene, it has to be treated with respect. Just a couple of questions that people have a right to ask: was this a commercial plane or private? What caused the crash and how many may have been on board?"

"No questions! Now if you'll get out of the way—"

"Was I in your way? Oh, I'm so sorry." Lila sounded genuinely distressed. She briefly rested her fingers on his arm. "Are you the head of the team? You have that sort of look about you." Taking a pencil from her handbag, she stuck out the pink tip of her tongue. Slowly licked the point of the pencil. Gave him a long look through tilted eyes as green as bottle glass.

Two minutes later he was spelling his name for her.

"Is that one *t* or two?" she queried. "My grandfather was Italian, he was another gorgeous man."

Surveying the wreckage piled up in Sycamore River, Edgar Tilbury mused upon how sad it was that someone would make a profit out of so much pain and loss.

"Life," he said aloud. "And death."

He took his AllCom from his pocket and made a call. "I need to talk to Bob Ferguson. That you, Bob? Ed Tilbury here. I've got another job for you in Sycamore River; demolition

and salvage this time. There's been a major disaster that needs
to be cleaned up as soon as possible. The mayor's office should
be taking care of this, but I suspect they're in shock themselves. Maybe some of them were among the victims. You get
yourself over here before the vultures start circling. If anyone
asks you for a work order, well, you know what to do."

He listened, nodding. Then grinned. "Sure I want a per-
centage if you can wheedle it out of the government!"


In its next edition *The Sycamore Seed* would inform its
readers:

> *In exclusive interviews with Mario Benedetti of
> the Federal Aviation Administration and Gerald
> Ashton from civil defense headquarters, this reporter
> learned the aircraft that caused devastation in Syca-
> more River on Sunday belonged to a small commer-
> cial airline. The plane was following an approved
> flight path along the Sycamore River Valley toward
> Benning. Preliminary investigation revealed the
> craft was not struck by a missile either foreign or
> domestic. No bomb or other incendiary device has
> been discovered in the wreckage. There was no fire
> until the fuel exploded on impact. More details may
> come to light when the inquests are complete. Mean-*

*while the cause of the disaster remains under investi-*
*gation.*

On Monday morning Lila put the completed article on Frank Auerbach's desk. He read it through twice, then gave her a quizzical look. "That's all you got?"

"All I've got for now, but both men said they'd keep in touch and inform me of developments."

"Lila, we can't leave our readers wondering what the hell happened. The first funerals will be—"

"I know. I saw the bodies." She stared over his head, trying not to remember.

"I'm counting on you for obits as soon as identifications are made."

She met his eyes. "I can't do it, Frank. I knew most of those people. Colin Bennett was my friend Nell's son and Bill Burdick and—"

"I knew 'em too; that's the curse of a town at a time like this. But because they were our friends we owe them our best efforts."

"Then you write their obituaries. I'm going home to get royally pissed."

The town was convulsed with grief and horror. Questions were on everyone's lips but there were no answers. Sycamore

River swarmed with officialdom also looking for answers, and embarrassed that they had none.

The impossible had happened.

For no apparent reason and without any warning, a well-maintained aircraft had simply disintegrated in midair.

Nell was inconsolable, but Jack was determined not to let another rift develop between them. He took her to Colin's funeral—the only one she could force herself to attend—then went home with her and slept on the couch in the living room. He was there for her when she woke up. To his surprise she emerged from her bedroom fully dressed and with her makeup neatly applied, though it could not disguise her red eyes. She went to the kitchen and insisted on preparing breakfast, though none of them were hungry.

"She's tougher than she looks," Tilbury had said.

When a storm of uncontrollable weeping swept over Jess, Jack was there for her too.

There were other funerals. His friends, his aunt's friends, people he had known for a long time and others he knew only on a professional basis. Bea's cardiologist and Jack's dentist and the tailor from the men's wear department at Goettinger's. Hooper Watson's widow Nadine, Arthur Hannisch, Martha Frobisher, the regular customers for the Sunday brunch. Familiar names and faces, people you'd stop to talk to on the sidewalk or in the barbershop because Sycamore River was a town, not a city.

Jack had always thought of himself as a lone wolf, yet

they were part of his personal history. Gone now. Wiped away.

Eternity was a black hole.

"It's just as well the crash happened on Sunday; otherwise we'd have lost the entire Wednesday Club," Jack said to Lila Ragland as they were leaving Sunnyslope Cemetery on a rainy afternoon. Behind them a mountain of flowers lent temporary life to the grave of Paige Prentiss.

Shay Mulligan was walking several paces behind them with his head down and his hands deep in his pockets. One on either side, Paige's parents were clutching his arms like drowning victims. They had traveled from Milwaukee and were gray with fatigue. They didn't plan to go back home for several days. Shay could not imagine what he was going to say or do to fill the time for them.

Lila said emphatically, "That was absolutely the last funeral I'm ever going to."

"What about your own?"

"I think I'll give it a miss."

Jack raised an eyebrow. "Plan to live forever, do you?"

"It beats the alternative."

"Then I hope there's something wonderful waiting for you in the future, Lila," he said sincerely.

"What happened to Paige's dog? I assume Shay put it to sleep."

"That's what he told her parents. They're in no condition to take Samson."

"You mean—"

Jack lowered his voice. "Ssshh, not so loud, they're right behind us. Shay was able to save him but he had to amputate the leg. A big strong dog like that, who's fighting so hard for his life; he has to have a chance."

"You're not going to take him, are you? I can't imagine Jack Reece tying himself down with a crippled dog."

"Guess what, Lila. I'm really tired of people thinking they know me."

# 12

The Wednesday Club would not be meeting at Bill's anymore. There was no bar and grill and no Bill Burdick either.

Six weeks after the last victim of the disaster was buried, Jack suggested that Bea Fontaine invite the surviving members of the club to meet in her house. "It'll be a relatively convenient location for everyone but Edgar Tilbury," he said, "and he'd come even if the meetings were on the moon."

"You think the club means that much to him? I suppose it does." Bea answered her own question. "An old man like that, living alone."

"He's not much older than you, Aunt Bea."

"Are you sure? He's certainly weathered. Perhaps I should have looked at his credit report when I was working in the bank."

"Why would you be interested?"

"I'm not."

The meeting would be well attended. The calamity had been so terrible, so incomprehensible, they needed to talk it out.

Bea spent the morning baking. Jack cruised through the kitchen at frequent intervals, licking bowls, tasting food, setting out drinks. His aunt had purchased a prodigious supply of liquid refreshment for her guests. "You've got enough booze here to last the rest of our lives," Jack said. "I'll have to stack the unopened cartons on the back porch."

"I didn't know what they'd ask for. I wish I'd paid more attention when we were at Bill's."

"It's okay, Aunt Bea; how could you know you'd be the next host? You should have called Lila and asked her; she notices details like that."

"Lila Ragland?"

"Who else?"

"Funny, I never thought of her."

"That's because you're a woman," Jack said.

He had called Nell twice to see if she wanted to join them; her answers had been so vague he did not try again. None of the others were surprised by her absence. Only Lila asked, "How's Nell bearing up since she lost Colin?"

Jack silently shook his head.

When the glasses had been refilled several times and the kitchen counters were stacked high with dirty dishes, the serious talking began.

"Can you imagine the nerve of that guy coming in with his bulldozers and dump trucks while the bodies were still warm in the morgue? Who sent for him, anyway?"

Edgar Tilbury silently studied his fingernails, then pulled out a handkerchief and vigorously applied it to his nose. He had been sneezing almost nonstop since he entered the house.

Someone said, "Mayor Dilworth must have arranged for the cleanup. I guess he wasn't as shell-shocked as he looked."

"No way; Do-Nothing Dilworth couldn't arrange three marbles in a bowl."

"Whoever it was, I'm grateful. The sight of that rubble . . ."

"It wasn't so bad after they took the corpses away."

"You see any corpses?"

"No. Well, maybe one. A piece of one. I lost my lunch."

Tilbury sneezed again. Bea gave him a sharp look. "Are you all right?"

"Cat allergy," he mumbled.

Gloria Delmonico said, "Oh, for heaven's sake, we have shots for that! Why don't you come in to the hospital?"

"Don't like hospitals. People die in hospitals." He stuffed his handkerchief back in his pocket.

"How the hell does a plane come apart like that? Has anybody figured it out yet?"

"If they had, the information would be in the paper by now," Lila responded. "Under my byline."

Evan said, "I'll bet Jack has a theory, he always does."

"Don't look at me, I'm giving up theorizing. I'm tired of being wrong so often."

"Hey, let's have another round of drinks; Jack Reece admits he's not an expert on everything."

Jack refused to be goaded. "The beginning of wisdom is admitting what you don't know. With the discovery of dark energy and dark matter scientists began to realize their ignorance. Thanks to space probes and powerful telescopes human knowledge currently extends to maybe four percent of the universe. Four percent! What about the rest?

"Does dark energy occupy seventy-two percent of the universe, as some of the best minds suggest? And if dark matter is invisible to the human eye and distorts light, then how can we measure it? Such a thing defies the laws of physics, which means they're not immutable after all. Other forces must be involved that we can't even guess at. We're like the blind men who touched the tip of an elephant's tail and thought they knew all there was to know about the animal."

Gerry Delmonico said, "What can we believe in, if not science?"

His wife cleared her throat. "You know what I believe in."

"Yeah, and it might have got you killed if you'd been sitting closer to that stained glass window."

Gloria gave her husband a frosty glare.

For the first time since the inception of the Wednesday Club the conversation deteriorated into a serious argument of science versus religion. This had been one topic they always avoided.

Unsuspected fault lines began to appear in the group.

Good thing Nell's not here after all, Jack thought. We might have found ourselves on opposite sides of a quarrel that can't be resolved.

The evening broke up early.

Edgar Tilbury was the last to leave; Jack was going to drive him home, since neither of them trusted his ancient pickup. Bea accompanied them as far as the front porch. The air was sodden with moisture. Tilbury commented, "It's frowning up to rain again, damn it. I'm sick to my back teeth of bad weather."

"I notice you didn't express any strong opinions during the argument tonight," said Bea.

"Neither did your nephew. What about it, Jack? Which do you believe in, God or science?"

"There was a time I would have answered without thinking twice, but dark energy rattled my cage. Let's say I plead ignorance in the absence of sufficient evidence."

Tilbury chuckled. "Coward."

"How about you?"

"I can see that we're going to have some stimulating conversations in my bolt-hole," Tilbury replied evasively.

"Who's on the guest list?" Bea asked.

He counted them off on his fingers. "You two of course; Nell Bennett, her mother and daughter; Shay and Evan Mulligan; Lila Ragland; the Delmonicos and their children, plus Bob and Mildred Ferguson and their two teenage daughters. That's all the people I've planned for. You don't know the Fergusons, they live in Nolan's Falls about forty miles north of here. They're not what I'd call close friends, but I owe Bob a favor from way back. He's a building contractor; handles all kinds of heavy equipment. They say his wife has a superb voice; she used to sing professionally before they married. She might even entertain us in the evenings if we ask her."

"You make doomsday sound like tomorrow."

"It almost is, Aunt Bea," Jack warned. "That airplane was just a curtain-raiser."

"How can you be sure?"

"If I tried to explain you wouldn't believe me."

Tilbury said to Bea, "This guy gets a real kick out of being mysterious, doesn't he?"

"It's his stock-in-trade. One of them," she amended.

"Predicting war isn't difficult," said Tilbury. "All you have to do is study the patterns of history and the way we humans work ourselves up for self-destruction time after time. In fact I'm afraid we're overdue."

Bea did not want to hear any more. "Take him home, Jack, before I shoot the messenger."


At the Staunton Memorial Hospital no one was shooting the messenger, but there was no enthusiasm for new patients. The facility was already over capacity. With some trepidation Gloria Delmonico brought Kirby Nyeberger to work with her one Thursday, hoping the new pain specialist would be able to give the boy some relief.

Of the five Nyeberger brothers, Kirby was the most intelligent. In other circumstances he might have been called gifted, but he had been through too much to have normal reactions. He oscillated between truculence and terror. Approaching the front door of the hospital was enough to make him tremble.

"This is going to be a good day," Gloria assured him. "You're not going to see the plastic surgeon at all." She gently took his claw of a hand in hers, but he pulled away.

"I won't go in there. If you try to make me I'll hit you."

"You won't hit me, Kirby; you never have. You're acting like a baby and you're not a baby, you're almost grown. We have a new doctor on staff who specializes in pain relief for burns like yours, and he—"

"Promise he's not going to touch me!"

"He can't help you if he doesn't touch you. I touch you sometimes, don't I? But I don't hurt you."

"It hurts like hell when you change dressings and the scab sticks."

"I know and I'm sorry, but that's part of the healing and this will be another part."

Behind Kirby's disfigured face, inside his maturing body, was a frightened child who had gone through hell and been emotionally stunted by it. Gloria spoke directly to that child. "Come with me now and I promise to give you a treat later."

He gave her a calculating look. "What kind of treat?"

"What would you like most?"

"I want more children," Gloria Delmonico told her husband. Taking advantage of a break in the weather he was raking dead leaves; she was kneeling beside her beloved iris bed, lifting and separating corms for the winter. She looked up at him and smiled invitingly.

Gerry propped the rake against the garden shed and pretended to unbutton his jeans. "Having a baby takes nine months as I recall. But if we start right now—"

"You goofball," she said fondly, "you know what I mean. I understand why our great-grandparents had so many children; they wanted to be sure they'd get to keep a few."

"Those were different times."

"They were, but bad things happened then too, just different bad things. This time an airplane crashed, next time it could be the space station or one of our satellites."

"I doubt it. Whatever's affecting metal doesn't seem to reach very far beyond Earth, Muffin."

"Then the next disaster could be the war everybody's expecting."

"It could be," he admitted. "Let's hope not. But children are hostages to fortune. You're worried about two now; you want to worry about three?"

"You're included in the number I worry about."

"I can take care of myself."

"I've never known a man who could take care of himself,"

Gloria said. "You just think you can. That's why God had to make women."

"And my woman wants another baby, so—"

"I said children, not a baby."

"What are you talking about?"

"I want to apply to the court for us to become foster parents for the Nyeberger orphans. Not Sandy, he's just joined the navy, but the four younger ones; Kirby in particular. I've got to know that boy. There's something special about him. I think I can bring it out, but I'll need to be with him more than a few hours a day. Those youngsters need a stable home with well-adjusted parents, otherwise what sort of men will they become? Imagine growing up with the knowledge that your mother was murdered by a stranger and your father went crazy and killed some other people."

"I'm sorry for them, I guess the whole town's sorry for them, Muffin. But I don't see anybody lining up to help them."

"We could. We *can*. We can apply to the Staunton Trust for sufficient money to keep the boys in our home until they're grown. If it's granted I could take an extended leave of absence to be with them."

Gerry was astonished. Obviously his wife already had everything worked out. Gloria had a habit of surprising him, it was one of the many reasons he loved her, but this one topped them all. "We have two children already," he said. "What makes you think the authorities would let us have four more?"

"Because the boys are in such desperate need. Nell Bennett

has a terrific lawyer, Finbar O'Mahony; he's represented her family for years. He tells me we'd have a good chance . . ." She took a deep breath and produced the ace from her sleeve. "And he's one of the Staunton trustees."

"Shouldn't you have talked to me first, Muffin? Now I don't know what to say."

She gave him a radiant smile. "Say yes."

As she looked down from her bench the judge forced a smile for Kirby Nyeberger. He could not reply in kind; normal facial expressions were impossible for him. Plastic surgery had mitigated some of the effects of his phosphorous burns and might make further improvements with time, but his mouth was still twisted to one side and the skin around his eyes was crumpled into folds. His thick black eyelashes extended from the lids like the legs of trapped insects.

The judge had to render a sensitive decision in a difficult case. Once the arrangement would have been unthinkable if not downright illegal, but fortunately the nation as a whole had outgrown racial prejudice. There were always a few, however, who hated blindly. Who knew what seeds had been sown in this tragic youngster?

"How would you feel," she asked, choosing her words carefully, "about living with persons of color?"

Bracketed by damaged eyelids, Kirby's eyes sparkled. "You

mean persons of color as compared to colorless persons? I'd choose the Delmonicos every time!"

"We have them!" a triumphant Gloria reported at the next meeting of the Wednesday Club. "There are still some papers to sign and we have to pick up their things from the Staunton house, but the Nyebergers are coming to us."

"I hope you're not going to regret this," said Jack.

"We probably will, a dozen times a day," Gerry replied. "But my wife's a mother hen. With a war coming she wants to get all the chicks under her wings."

"I never thought of Gloria as a mother hen. She looks like a fashion model."

"That's what I did in college," she told Jack, "before I began studying psychology. Gerry and I both come from big families and wanted to have our own, but it took years before I finally conceived our two. The doctors tell me it won't happen again, but now our family is complete." Her happiness filled the room.

Bea went to her refrigerator and took out the two bottles of champagne she kept at the very back for special occasions. As she handed them to Jack to open she said very softly, "A ready-made family isn't such a bad thing."

———

The war was coming. Even the most determined optimist could not ignore the signs. Sandy Nyeberger was only one of many Sycamore River boys, and quite a few girls, who were looking forward to a career in the armed forces.

But not Colin, Nell thought as she lay awake at three in the morning and listened to the beating of her heart. *My poor Colin never had his chance. He would have chosen to die on the battlefield, a hero like his father. In spite of what the town thought about him, Robert Bennett had pulled one of the Nyeberger boys out of the flames in the factory at the cost of his own life.*

Nell took her husband's framed photo from the drawer in her bedside table and studied the belligerent features, the pugnacious jaw. "You *were* a hero," she whispered to him.

She put the photo back in the drawer and forced herself to think about something else; a happy thought to soothe her to sleep. The wedding date was set and the arrangements confirmed. Not tomorrow, nor next week, but when Colin's death was just far enough in the past to make the occasion bearable; even necessary. Life going on, and all that. Nell was having a new dress made for the occasion, which was another reason for the delay. The best dressmaker in Sycamore River said, "You want it fast or you want it good?"

Katharine Richmond continued to complain because the wedding would not take place in a chapel. "A chapel wedding implies a belief in God and I don't have one, not anymore," Nell told her.

"Jack Reece put you up to this, didn't he?"

"It wasn't his idea, but he'll go along with whatever I want. You don't have to come to the wedding if it upsets you so much. You know where the registrar's office is; you can meet us there at two in the afternoon, three weeks from today. Or not," Nell added with a stubborn tilt to her chin.

# 13

Beneath the cold waters of the Atlantic burned a nuclear heart. The submarine, fitted for silent running, came as close to the continental shelf as possible. The commander had made many of these cruises from Greenland to the Bahamas. Other submariners were reconnoitering the Pacific coast. Their vessels were capable of staying submerged twenty-four hours a day, seven days a week, as long as necessary. The recently developed technique of extracting their oxygen directly from the water gave them a great advantage.

Eyes in the ocean, eyes in the sky.

A little spark was all that was needed; one could come from anywhere. A diplomatic miscalculation, a garbled word, a misunderstood command. The whole world was a tinderbox and the international armaments industry was waiting for an instigator.

One angry man had been responsible for the disastrous Charge of the Light Brigade.

One angry man had fired the shot that had started World War One.

When the commander of the submarine in the Atlantic discovered his vessel was in trouble, he could hardly believe it.

She was the pride of the fleet, impervious to the sea and superbly armored, capable of launching missiles equipped with nuclear warheads. How could she possibly be disintegrating?

Fury broke out in the most recent iteration of the United Nations. Delegate after delegate in the main chamber accused the Americans of industrial sabotage on an unprecedented scale. Military hardware had begun falling apart. Rivets tore loose, steel buckled. Not only airplanes and submarines but also tanks and battleships were disintegrating. The same fate was occurring to missiles with or without warheads, incendiary devices of every description and all forms of artillery. Item by item, the munitions essential for war were turning into scrap.

The representative for the United States argued that the same misfortune was befalling his country's arsenals. He had photographs to prove what he said; he waved them in the air in front of his opposite number across the table. Who insisted that the American lied. The Yankees always lied, everyone knew it.

Voices were raised to the decibel level of a train wreck; a battlefield.

The only thing worse than waging war, it seemed, was losing the weapons to wage war.

Never in the checkered history of the United Nations had so much rage been expended within the chamber. Men and women were clambering over their desks to attack other men and women. An emergency summons brought the sergeants at arms, who were soon fighting one another.

There was blood on the floor.

Lila Ragland put her hands palm down on Frank Auerbach's cluttered desk and leaned toward him to make her point. "You heard me; we're on the verge of total war and there's every indication it will be nuclear. Too many nations have that capability now. We kept coming close and then backing up, but sooner or later someone was bound to reach for the nukes."

"I know." He sounded defeated. "We'd better get out a special edition, Lila."

She straightened up. "If our machinery fails we're not going to be able to produce the *Seed* at all; not unless you expect me to write every newspaper in longhand. In that case you can consider this my resignation."

His watery eyes threatened to overflow. "I couldn't possibly accept it, you know how I rely on you. Besides, didn't you tell me the metal failures were random? 'Sporadic,' I think that was the word you used. That's how it was with plastic too." He added hopefully, "Maybe whatever-it-is won't have any effect on our presses."

"You're whistling past the graveyard, Frank. The whole thing's started over again with a different target, that's all.

And metal that falls apart is a lot more serious than dissolving plastic."

"I suppose you're going to say no one knows the cause this time either."

"That's right. According to my sources . . . which are getting harder to contact, by the way . . . the scientists are tying themselves in knots but can't come up with any answers. All they know is it's happening to alloyed metals, not pure metal."

"Well then, why can't—"

"Because the metals we use are all made with alloys. They'd be too soft otherwise."

He looked shocked. "My wife's jewelry is solid gold! I should know, I paid for it; she won't wear anything but eighteen karat."

"Sorry, Frank, but you're wrong. It can be legally sold as gold, but it's only eighteen karats of gold and six karats of a different metal."

"Even her wedding ring?"

Lila nodded.

"I have to go home and tell Janice her wedding ring's going to—"

Lila nodded again.

Frank Auerbach was not used to being helpless. This reminded him of the queasy sensation he had when he awoke in the morning with the sure knowledge that he would die someday and there was nothing he could do about it. "If you're right, Lila, we're facing a bleak future. It's just not possible."

"I used to think a lot of things were impossible but I was wrong. Time to reset, Frank."

"How are you going to do that?"

She took Tilbury's homemade AllCom from her pocket. "Communicate."

When Tilbury's call registered on his AllCom Jack answered immediately. The rusty voice began without preamble. "It's starting. I just heard from Lila; she has sources everywhere. She says the UN is bracing for a declaration of war any day now. The military chiefs want to use their weapons before the damned things disintegrate."

"But we're getting married!" Jack protested, then laughed at how ridiculous he sounded.

In spite of the gravity of the situation Tilbury chuckled too. "Maybe I better invite a clergyman to join us in the bolt-hole."

Even if it might never be printed, Lila struggled to write an informative article that could help Sycamore River readers understand what was happening without causing panic. She was walking a tightrope on a very thin rope.

Give them the bad news first, she decided, then slip the

really bad news in at the end, the way politicians do on Friday night.

Her headline read simply:

## NEW CRISIS

*Ever since 9/11 an effort has been made to replace steel with a more fire-resistant material, but structural steel continues to support buildings on every continent. It is still used in not only skyscrapers but also offices, hospitals, high-rise apartments, any multistory construction. Thin strips of steel also are embedded in concrete blocks to reinforce their weight-carrying ability. Steel frames hold reinforced glass panels attached to the outside of buildings as rigid cladding for added support.*

*Steel is under attack in every country. Buildings are beginning to lose their structural integrity. We are advised to be suspicious of any structure we enter. At the Salk Institute for Biological Studies in Spain a top-secret laboratory, jointly funded by the US and the EU, has collapsed, crushing the entire team of scientists at work on the so-called immortality gene.*

*Also failing are the highly detailed models based on algorithms that are used by industrial contractors to promote their projects. The era of computational architecture using nano structures of steel is ending almost as soon as it began.*

*During the Change we discovered how dependent we had become on plastic. Now we are facing the worldwide disintegration of metal. The effect on the weapons industry is bringing us to the brink of war. Nations rely on their military forces and the military relies on its firepower. With the loss of munitions the balance of power becomes unstable. In this new crisis of uncertainty we must be prepared for the worst.*

When Lila put the typewritten article on Frank Auerbach's desk he skimmed the text, then read it word for word, silently moving his lips. He scowled up at her. "What do you mean, 'be prepared'?"

"It's up to each person to figure that out for themselves, I guess."

"Oh, great. You think we should run articles on civil defense and bomb shelters?"

"I can research them if I have time."

"What the hell does that mean?" Auerbach added the article to the papers in his in-box. "Lila, sometimes I think you're more trouble than you're worth."

"Just consider me an early warning system."

That night Lila took carbon copies of her article to the next meeting of the Wednesday Club and passed them around.

"You won't be reading this in the *Seed* because we're not publishing anymore. Our presses are kaput; this is a once-in-a-lifetime collectors' issue."

When Jack finished reading the article he asked, "Is this true, about the Salk Institute? Were they really working on an immortality gene?"

"Apparently so, but their lab was destroyed along with the men and women in it. There's nothing left of the project unless they had duplicate records somewhere else."

"I sure hope somebody finds them," said Evan Mulligan.

"I don't think we're meant to be immortal," Bea told him. "Right now you may like the idea but I don't want to be a hundred years old; living in a ramshackle body would take the pleasure out of life."

"But if your body stayed young too—"

"Did you ever read *Peter Pan*? In it Peter says, 'Dying must be an awfully big adventure!'"

"Easy for him to talk," Evan retorted. "Peter Pan was immortal, wasn't he?"

"I'm not sure, I'd have to reread the book again; right now I'm more concerned about what happens to metal. This is a frame house, I doubt if there's any structural steel in it. I do have beautiful cast-iron radiators, though; they're part of the period fittings. What about them, Jack; are they going to fall apart on me?"

"Gerry has a friend named Erasmus Barber who's a metallurgist. He'd be the one to ask."

Tilbury said, "Gerry could put you in touch with him, but the Delmonicos aren't here tonight; anyone know why?"

"Four good reasons," Nell replied. "Kirby, Brewster, Philip and Daniel. The Delmonicos are staying at home to help the Nyeberger boys get settled in."

"How many kids did you say?"

"Four boys, Edgar. You can accommodate them, can't you? You said your friends the Fergusons have two daughters."

"I wasn't planning to breed humans, damnit!"

Jack looked from one person to the next. Anxiety was visible on every face but no one seemed willing to make the next move. At this penultimate moment, asking to enter the shelter was a step too far; it would make the nightmare real. "Come on, Edgar," he urged, "it sounds like we might be running out of time."

Tilbury turned toward Lila. "Are we? Is it that close?"

"I think so. It can't be more than a few days. If I can get away with it I'm going to sneak our shortwave system out of the newspaper office and bring it to you."

Tilbury tugged thoughtfully at his earlobe. Every person in the room knew about the refuge and had been included in his plans. His future plans.

The future was now.

All right.

"When do you want to come for a holiday at my place?" he asked the room at large. "The sooner the better, we don't want to cut this too fine."

"How long should we be prepared to stay?"

"Months, unless we're either lucky or very unlucky. Bring your important documents: birth certificates, passports, wills, deeds, stocks and bonds . . . though who knows what those'll be worth when this is over. Include your good jewelry if it's still holding together, and any gold coins you've been hiding to keep them from Internal Revenue. Find a drugstore and refill your prescriptions as far ahead as the doctors will let you; say you're going on a world cruise. I have plenty of first aid supplies and a defibrillator; I'm the oldest person in the group so I want to be sure the rest of you know how to use one."

That man's clever, Jack thought; he's giving them something to concentrate on to distract them from their fear. He took out his AllCom. "Before you go into any more details, Edgar, I'm recording this so everyone can have a copy."

Tilbury nodded approval. "It's not cold underground," he continued, "but we can't predict what the weather will be like when we come out. Think about what global warming's done to us, and I don't mean just the epidemic of hurricanes and earthquakes. Be prepared with both summer and winter clothes, warm nightwear, a heavy coat and several pairs of shoes. Sturdy shoes," he stressed, looking at Nell, "and thick socks. Don't forget your toiletries—soap, toothbrushes and toothpaste, deodorant . . . plenty of deodorant. We'll take showers to conserve water.

"You'll sleep in small chambers in the tunnels, like the

sleeping pods in Japanese hotels. They'll provide an added layer of protection. They're equipped with air mattresses and a pump to inflate them. It's about as much privacy as you'd find in a Pullman car on an old-fashioned train, but you won't be uncomfortable. Just don't thrash around in your sleep. The sanitation is adequate but it's not luxurious either . . ."

Jack's attention was wandering. The minutiae of life, he thought; the mundane details that underpin our existence. Arranging dental appointments, getting a haircut. Paying taxes. The blueprint for civilization. Now it's being stripped away and we're left with a struggle for basic survival.

To hell with toothpaste.

Tilbury was saying, "Bring any medications your pets may need too. And flea powder; we don't want any unwelcome company."

"Where are we going to put this stuff, Edgar?"

"There's enough room down below, don't worry."

"You must have spent a fortune fitting out the place."

"I did, but I'm not running a charitable institution."

Jack waited until the others were engaged in conversation, then sidled up to Tilbury. "What did you mean by that crack about not running a charitable institution?"

"Just what I said. I originally built the shelter for myself, but since it's been stocked to accommodate a crowd I'm going to insist the crowd shares the expenses."

"You old dog! When do you plan to tell them?"

"When they're snugged in tight and safe and the bombs are falling. I don't think anyone will refuse me then, do you?"

"I misjudged you, Edgar."

Tilbury smiled. "Everyone does."

"Atom bombs. Or hydrogen bombs. You were damned smart to buy property out in the country far away from any potential ground zero. If there's fallout at least we'll be underground. Let me ask you something else, Edgar. You know much about drone technology?"

"I'm a dedicated tinkerer, Jack."

"Then have you ever seen a midsize drone that attracts Saint Elmo's fire?"

Tilbury frowned. "I suppose one could, under the right conditions. What's this all about?"

"I'm wondering just who or what we're going to be fighting."

# 14

When the last of the Wednesday Club had departed Jack refilled his tumbler of Irish whiskey. To the brim. He sat down in his favorite armchair and leaned his head against the back. He was weary past weariness, yet still taut with tension.

"That's it, Aunt Bea. Starting tomorrow we'll begin shuttling people out to Edgar's as soon as they're ready. I'd like to have them all there by Monday. We're short on motorized transport but I'll take you in my car first, then come back for Nell and Jess."

"Take them first, Jack, she's your—"

"Let me do the prioritizing. You've been my family all my life and those cats are your family, so I'll take them too. Don't argue. I just wish I'd bought a larger car. My last run will be for Nell's mother. Her arthritis is getting bad but she won't admit it; I'll see if I can pick up a walker for her, maybe a folding wheelchair.

"The Fergusons will be driving down from Nolan's Falls in their own car. Gerry keeps the horse-bus and team at his place; in addition to his family it can carry pets and luggage. Evan can take Lila and Shay in the cart along with his veterinary supplies."

"Trap, not cart," Bea corrected her nephew. "That sort of small cart's known as a pony-and-trap, except Rocket's a horse and not a pony. Haven't you noticed that Evan's particular about such things?"

"This is no time for nitpicking, Aunt Bea. We're going to be living cheek by jowl for the foreseeable future, so we better not be too touchy."

"Speak for yourself."

"What's that supposed to mean?"

"You have the hottest temper of anyone in town, Jack. Most of the time you keep a lid on it, but I know you. If you insist that everything be done your way you're going to have a mutiny on your hands. This would be a bad time for it."

He took a deep drink of whiskey and closed his eyes. "Who died and made you God?"

"No one, but you're not God either. I'm just telling you." She began bustling around the room, collecting used glasses and plates, wadding up paper napkins. She did not look at him again.

He watched her through slitted eyelids but made no move to help; a small and silent war that could not be won but must not be lost. They were both familiar with the unspoken rules that shaped their lives together.

At last Bea remarked, "I don't suppose I'll need to contact that metal expert—what was his name, Erasmus something?—about my radiators."

"Overtaken by events," Jack said tersely.

When Jack's AllCom alerted him it dragged him out of a deep and troubled sleep. He took the device from beneath his pillow and propped it up on the nightstand, so he could keep an eye on the illuminated time.

Six thirty. On a winter morning. As dark as the inside of a rock.

Shit.

Lila's voice was familiar but the face on the screen was pale and haggard. "They're coming from the south," she said, "and it looks like they'll pass right over Sycamore River."

"They who?" He felt groggy and there was a headache starting behind his eyes. "What do you mean?"

"Bombers, with a large fighter escort. They're flying up from South America. We thought the attack would begin with missiles on the West Coast, but the planes are headed for the middle of the country. And troopships are reported sailing toward Bermuda, which must mean they'll disembark in Florida. There were some other details being broadcast but the shortwave's mostly static now. They're jamming it."

Jack was instantly, painfully awake. "Damn the man to hell!" he exploded. "We've got to contact everyone *now*. I hope they went home last night and started getting ready, but we're overtaken by events. Murphy's Law will destroy the human race if we give it a chance. Have you called anyone else?"

"Edgar was the first, then you."

"Okay; I'll contact Gerry and Evan and get them going. If we're really lucky we just might make it."

"Do you want me to . . ." But Jack was already out of bed, pulling on a thick Aran sweater and heavy jeans.

Bea was standing in the door of her bedroom, rubbing her eyes. "Who were you swearing at?"

"The deranged politician who alienated our southern neighbors years ago. We're under attack, Aunt Bea, and it sounds like those same neighbors are allied with our enemies now."

"Surely not!"

"Don't be surprised. Look at the way Europe split after Queen Victoria died. We don't have time to discuss history; pack your things and collect your cats, we'll be making a trip to the country."

While she complied Jack phoned Gerry and Evan, then Nell.

Who promptly phoned her mother.

Katharine Richmond took the news badly. She broke into such a flood of weeping that Nell could not make her understand.

"It's the end of the world, it's Armageddon! The Bible said it would happen in the Mideast but—"

"It's not Armageddon, Mom; we're going to be all right. Can you hear me? We'll be just fine, we're going to a safe place in the country. Jack will take us."

"I'm not going anywhere, I'm staying here in Sycamore

River with your father. I'll go to the cemetery and lie on his grave until—"

"*Please,* Mom, listen to me! You're getting hysterical."

The sun was not yet awake; it slumbered below the horizon. Only a faint hint of cold light had crept into a sky pregnant with clouds. "Snow clouds," Bea Fontaine commented when she looked out the kitchen window. "You'd better hurry up and finish eating," she warned her cats. "Jack says we're leaving in fifteen minutes."

Before she left the house Bea opened a suitcase and took out a heavy wool coat to wrap around herself. On the front porch she paused; trailed her fingers along the back of a wicker chair. Patted the porch railing. "A glass of iced tea," she murmured to herself, "on a hot summer day."

She had turned on the porch light; she waited while Jack backed his car out of the garage.

The little coupé would be crowded with two grown adults and seven cats in wicker carriers, but Bea would not put the cats in the trunk. "They'd be scared shut up in the dark. I was going to get a couple of large wire cages for them that you could have tied on the roof, but the pet shop didn't have any wire cages. They didn't even have any stainless-steel feeding bowls left. It's like plastic all over again."

Jack seated his aunt, stowed her suitcases in the trunk

and wedged the wicker cat carriers into the front. As they set off he heard one small miaow of protest, followed by silence.

"They're taking it surprisingly well," he said.

"So far. Cats are good at reading a situation; if they thought it would benefit them they'd complain, but maybe they recognize how serious this is."

"Wait till they find out they're going to be living with dogs."

Bea said, "At least they'll have a little time to get settled in before the dogs arrive."

As they drove out of town they saw other refugees in the gray and grainy light. Those who still had operative automobiles were driving them. Some people had horse-drawn carts or buggies; others were riding horseback or mounted on bicycles. Men and women on foot were hurrying along the road with their sleepy children in tow.

"Jack, can we take those children?"

"There isn't enough room in the car, Aunt Bea, and I doubt if their parents would let a couple of strangers have them. Besides, Edgar's not planning on any more people."

"But children, Jack!"

He did not reply. He tried not to see the resemblance between the people of Sycamore River and ants fleeing a disturbed nest.

When Jack stopped his car in front of Tilbury's house

Edgar came out to meet them, accompanied by a large three-legged black dog. The dog greeted the car with a bark of challenge.

Inside their wicker cases the cats hissed back at him.

Jack pressed a button and lowered a window. Cold winter air blew into the car. The cat who had complained before did so again.

"I didn't know you had a dog, Edgar," Bea said.

"This is Samson; he belonged to Shay's nurse at the clinic. When Lila brought Shay out here to view the facilities they brought the dog along; Shay thought it would do him good to have room to run, encourage him to move again. He and I took a liking to each other and he stayed. Two banged-up old codgers together." Tilbury bent and peered into the crowded interior of the car. "How many cats do you have there, Bea?"

"Seven."

"Seven. Well, the Delmonicos have six kids now, so I guess that's okay. Jack, drive around to the barn so you can unload; I know you're in a hurry to go back to town for Nell and her family."

"You sure it's safe to leave my aunt alone with you?"

"Absolutely not!"

Jack had never seen Bea blush before; he would have thought she was too old.

By the time the cats and Bea's luggage had been carried into the barn, the wintry light was growing weaker rather than stronger, as if the clouds were crouching low to protect the earth. Bea was relieved when Tilbury switched on the electric lights. "Here you are," he said heartily. "All the comforts of home, just down those stairs. Come with me and I'll show you where your room is; I guess you want to share it with the cats?"

"Of course. Apollo and Plato always sleep with me at night."

"Uh-huh."

On the drive back to Sycamore River Jack broke the speed limit all the way. He had disconnected the warning voice before he left home.

Nell and Jess were waiting for him at their front door. The two Irish setters frisked around them, excited. "If they'll ride in the trunk of the car we can take them now," Jack said, "but if not, I'll pick them up when I come back to town for . . ." He stopped when he saw the look on Nell's face.

"My mother told me she won't come."

"Of course she'll come. Did you explain the arrangements to her?"

"I couldn't make her listen to me, she wasn't making sense herself. She said she was going out to Sunnyslope to wait on my father's grave."

"Wait for what?"

"The end of the world. Then she switched off that old All-Com of hers and I couldn't get any answer from her."

God, I don't need this. "Jess, help me put your dogs in the trunk," Jack said, "and we'll drive by Katharine's apartment first. If she's not there we'll swing by the cemetery, it's on our way out of town. Meanwhile I'll phone Gerry to keep an eye out for her and pick her up if he sees her."

The dogs put up a fight. Jack came within a hair's breadth of leaving them behind but forced the issue and slammed the lid.

The women rode beside him with their suitcases piled on their laps, partially obscuring his view. He found it even more uncomfortable than carrying Bea's cats.

When they reached Katharine Richmond's apartment the door was unlocked but she was not inside. Nell ran from room to room, then returned to Jack with tears in her eyes. "How could Mom do this to us? How *could* she?"

"She probably wasn't thinking about us at all. Maybe she persuaded one of her neighbors to take her to Sunnyslope," Jack said hopefully.

Mrs. Richmond was not at the cemetery either. The only thing on her husband's grave was a vase of flowers his wife had left there the week before. The first snowflakes were settling on dying roses.

Precious minutes were ticking by.

"I'll wait for you in the car," Jack told Nell. "You and Jess might want a couple minutes of privacy; just don't take long."

Nell removed the roses from the vase and laid them on the earth like a tribute. It felt as if the dying had already begun. Nothing remained but the acceptance. There would be time enough for that later; now tribute must be paid to life.

She put an arm around her daughter's shoulders. "Let's go to Tilbury's."

They walked to the car in silence. Neither looked back. The two women squeezed into their seats and took their suitcases onto their laps. Nell asked Jack, "What happens now?"

"While I was waiting for you I looked at my AllCom; I don't know how up-to-date the news reporting is but some is still coming through, so the satellite service is working. There's a lot of interference with it and some of the transmissions are garbled. The enemy planes could be almost here, or they could be meeting resistance from our air force. I just don't understand why they're targeting the middle of the country."

A muffled voice said from behind the suitcases, "Colin told me—"

"What's that, Jess?"

"Colin told me there's a secret military facility on the old RobBenn land. They're experimenting with a new super-weapon out there."

Nell said, "How could he know that?"

"He'd been out there. He thought he'd be one of the men using it."

Bea looked at the luggage and cat cases stacked at the top of the stairs in the barn. "Edgar, we should have asked Jack to help us carry these down."

"He had to get back to town pronto."

"I understand, but . . . I wish he was still here. I probably rely on him too much but it's gotten to be a habit."

"Who does he rely on?"

She gave Tilbury a surprised look. "I never thought of that."

"You'll miss him once he's married."

"No! I mean no, I won't, I'll be happy for him."

"Life's never that simple, Bea, and neither are emotions. Things are always simmering under the surface. S'pose I told you that . . . dog! Stop sniffing those cats!"

Samson was a good dog and he tried to obey, but he was awkward after his amputation. When he jumped away he knocked over the stack of wicker carriers.

Seven cats escaped and ran off in seven directions.

# 15

Jack was worried by the heavy overcast. The enemy might be anywhere above them. Bombers had to reach a prescribed altitude before they dropped their bombs, but what about other forms of aircraft? Could he hear a missile coming? He lowered his window, but the only sound was the rushing of air.

"Are you trying to freeze us?"

"Sorry, Jess. I was just listening—"

"For a drone and a purple light?" Nell asked.

"Funny you should mention that. Did you ever tell Colin about what we saw?"

"It made me too uneasy. He'd been talking about joining the military so he could work with drones . . . then a few days later he was . . . no, I never told Colin about what we saw."

"I shouldn't have reminded you."

"No, it's all right," Nell said. Jack knew it wasn't.

He sought to mollify her. "Colin was a bright boy and he was interested in drones; I'd have liked to hear his ideas. Strange things are going on and I have a feeling they're connected, but I don't know how."

"We're being invaded, that's enough," Nell said sharply. "Won't this car go any faster?"

"Jack's got it wide open now," said Jess. "He's doing his best, Mom."

If he could have seen around the piled luggage Jack would have thrown her a grateful look.

Beneath a lowering sky, the blue coupé sped on.

When the sonic boom came it was like a clap of thunder. Jess gasped.

A white rail fence on one side of the road shuddered violently.

"Too low," Jack said through gritted teeth.

"What's too low?"

"The plane that just broke the sound barrier, Nell. Going that fast this close to the earth . . ." He tightened his grip on the steering wheel, bracing himself for the crash.

There was none.

Jack had a mental image of the hidden sky swarming with murderous machines.

The dogs in the trunk of the car were scratching wildly to get out.

"Nell, take my AllCom out of my jacket pocket and call the starred numbers. It's the list for the shelter. Find out where they are and if they're okay."

He kept his hands on the steering wheel while she made the calls. "Your aunt and Edgar are fine," she reported, "but he says they had cat trouble. The cats got out while they were being unloaded. Edgar doesn't sound very happy about it; I guess he's not familiar with cats. Evan's almost there with his father and Lila . . . and Karma, I can hear her yowling. Gerry's got his wife and all their kids; they're just turning off the main road." Nell pressed a button, waited, tried again. "There's no answer from the Fergusons."

"They'll be driving down from Nolan's Falls; even allowing for traffic it won't take an hour. Try them again in a little while."

"They're the couple with two children, aren't they?"

Jack's knuckles were white on the wheel. "Yes."

"Mom's not answering either," Nell said.

They heard another sonic boom in the distance.

Looking to his left, Jack saw a dark smudge where the land met the sky. Above it, flashes of pink and orange light appeared through a veil of black clouds.

The scene was malevolent.

What had Edgar called them? "Deranged politicians and professional hate mongers." They were worse than that. Those who had precipitated the dreadful spectacle were emotionally stunted megalomaniacs playing a monstrous game with the lives of everything on earth.

The headache pounding behind his eyes expanded to fill his whole skull.

"Are we almost there?"

"We've made good time, Nell. We'll leave the main road in a couple of minutes."

"I'm glad; the light is so peculiar now . . ." She gave a nervous laugh. "I want to crawl into Edgar's bolt-hole and pull it in after me."

"Are we really going to be safe there, Mom? Don't lie to me."

"I don't lie to you, Jess. Well, hardly ever; parents are entitled to a little fib every now and then."

"Will Evan be there too?"

"We might actually pass him on the road," Jack interjected. "Look ahead there . . . no, it's Gerry with the horse-bus." Relief washed over him. "I'm like Gloria, I'll be glad when all the chicks are under my wings."

He tapped the car's horn. Gerry looked back and waved.

Nell's eyes searched the crowded carriage, hoping against hope. But Katharine Richmond was not among the passengers.

Following close behind the horse-bus, the blue coupé turned off the main road, drove over a rusty iron cattle guard and jolted down a rutted laneway. The fields on either side were pastureland sparsely studded with boulders. After a few hundred yards the lane curved to the right. The view ahead was blocked by a dense stand of cedars, a menacing army in the strange light. Beyond them a rambling white frame farmhouse nestled amid unpruned shrubbery. On a hill at the far end of the property stood a massive barn.

Following the horse-bus, Jack circled around the house and drove to the barn. The pony-and-trap were already there.

Jess extricated herself from the coupé and ran to meet Evan. He folded her into his arms and lowered his face to kiss the top of her head.

Gerry handed his wife down from the horse-bus. She was carrying their little son in her arms. "We made it," Gloria said breathlessly.

"Just in time," Edgar told them. "Everyone go into the barn, will you? I'll guide you from there."

Jess looked at the mountain of stuff still piled in the horse-bus. "What's all that?" she asked Evan. "Does it go inside?"

Kirby Nyeberger answered her question. "When they showed natural disasters on the wallscreen people were always looking for blankets, so I stripped the beds and the linen closet in our house and brought all we had. And the pillows."

"Good thinking," she said as she turned toward him. Then she saw his face. Jess had never seen Kirby before. She could not help staring for a horrified moment before she looked away.

Kirby was staring at her too. In adolescence he had never seen a pretty girl who wasn't a nurse at the hospital and associated with pain. When he saw how quickly Jess turned away he discovered a new kind of pain.

"There's no response from the Fergusons," Jack was saying to Tilbury. "Are you sure their AllCom's working?"

"I made it for them myself. But anything could have happened; maybe they broke it or lost it or—"

"Anything could have happened," Jack echoed. "Maybe your friend forgot to get a full charge in his car last night."

"It shouldn't make any difference, there are charging stations all along the interstate."

"Coming out of town we saw people one step short of running for their lives," Jack replied. "Nobody's very organized this morning."

"He is," Jess said, indicating Kirby. "He brought all the blankets and pillows from home."

When he looked at her this time she met his eyes unflinchingly. And smiled.

Jack and Tilbury opened the large front doors of the barn so Gerry could drive the carriage inside. Evan followed with the trap. Jack maneuvered his car onto a patch of remaining floor space just inside the front doors. After he got out he walked around the coupé several times, looking closely for any sign of disintegration. He saw none. Yet. He extended his scrutiny to the farm machinery and Tilbury's battered old pickup truck. None of them appeared to have been affected.

Was there something special about the barn that kept them protected? Or was it merely coincidence?

Evan had begun unharnessing the horses. While they were outside they had been nervous, but once the doors closed behind them and they were in the stalls they began to relax.

People, animals, luggage . . . the barn embraced them all.

"This is a funny sort of Noah's Ark," remarked Brewster Nyeberger.

Gerry said, "Millions of people would like to have one just like it, Buster."

"I'm not the only survivalist in the country," Tilbury told them. "There are thousands of us scattered all over the map; some alone, some with their families or living in groups. They're mostly in isolated places rather than in cities. A city's the most dangerous place to be during a catastrophe. Too many things can burn or explode or kill you one way or another, and too many people want to survive instead of you. In a panic, they'll step on you and never look back. When it's over, and it will be over, the plain folks like you and me will come popping out of their holes to see what's left."

"I'm glad war's finally been declared," Lila said fiercely. "The waiting was the worst, like waiting for the guillotine blade to fall. That must have seemed to take an eternity for the poor wretch being executed. Once the worst happens there's nothing left to be scared of."

Jack responded, "The worst hasn't happened yet; we may have a long wait for it. We might as well go below, Nell, and . . . Nell?" He looked anxiously around the barn. "Nell!"

He ran to the side door and threw it open.

She was standing there, gazing toward the orange light and boiling cloud. "If it's going to kill me," she said in a calm voice, "I want to have a good look at it first."

She was wearing her Joan of Arc face again. Suddenly he knew how very much he loved her.

"You're not afraid, are you?"

"To die? I faced the fact a long time ago that death is inevitable. The circumstances matter, though. I don't want to die without putting up a good fight."

He started to put an arm around her and pull her to him, then thought better of it. This was a woman who could stand on her own. He stood next to her without saying anything until she turned to go back into the barn.

They went in together.

# 16

For the Nyeberger twins, Tilbury's refuge was the most exciting place they could imagine. "It's better than a pirate cave, even!" They could not be still for a minute; they wanted to explore every inch of it. Go down every tunnel, open every door.

Flub and Dub were identical. They not only looked alike and sounded alike—even their birth mother, Patricia Staunton Nyeberger, had never been able to tell which one was talking—but they also had similar thought patterns. When they got into trouble it was always in tandem.

Flub, the elder of the pair by eight minutes, had been so traumatized by the disaster at RobBenn that for a time he had lost the power of speech. Once he started talking again he hardly ever stopped—except to allow enough time for Dub to agree with him.

Like many identical twins they had created their own mythology. Shortly after they came to live with the Delmonicos Flub had tried to explain it to Gloria. Who had tried to explain it to Gerry.

Who had decided something was being lost in the translation.

"You mean they think they're immortal, Muffin?"

"Oh no. But one can't die."

"Which one?"

"Both of them."

"Say what?"

"They believe they're both the same person, Gerry. If one dies the *person* goes on living in the other one."

"That's crazy."

"Not to the boys; it's their faith. Faith is different things to different people."

Gloria recalled that conversation as she made her careful way down the stairs to the shelter, carrying her little son in her arms. Gerry had taken their daughter first, and the twins were already below. She could hear their whoops of excitement as they ran up one tunnel and down another.

While she was packing their things earlier Flub had asked her why such a refuge was necessary.

Gloria had been unsure how much of the truth to share with him; Flub was a damaged child. Already she loved him; loved them both. They had skinny necks and jug handle ears and an incorrigible propensity for mischief that was oddly innocent, because they never meant to do harm. They were always surprised when their adventures turned out badly.

She had asked Flub, "Remember those awful storms that flood the southern states every year?"

"Sure. Our teacher in school said it was because of global

warming and we'd gone past the 'tipping point,' whatever that is, and could never go back."

"The people who left the Gulf Coast area for good were evacuating, Flub. It means getting out of harm's way. That's what we're going to do now."

"Is there going to be a ji-*normous* storm?" he had asked hopefully.

"I'm afraid so."

"Then can't we stay here and see it? Nothing can hurt Dub and me, I 'splained about that."

"We have to go," she said firmly. "The rest of us don't have your—"

"Magical skills," he had finished for her. "Okay, let's go, we don't want anything bad to happen to you and Gerry."

They were still Gloria and Gerry to the Nyeberger boys. The couple hoped someday—Gloria in particular hoped— they would be Mom and Dad. In the meantime they would have preferred to drop the twins' nicknames in favor of their real ones, Philip and Daniel.

But the Delmonicos already had a daughter named Danielle.

Gerry had suggested, "Let's let the kids work it out for themselves; they probably will anyway."

Gloria reached the bottom of the stairs with a sigh of relief. When she was a teenager she had fallen down a steep flight of steps and fractured several vertebrae. Persistent nightmares about falling eventually led to her studying psychology—but she would never be comfortable on stairs.

Dub called out, "Hey Flub, c'mere, there's lots of cats in here! Help me catch 'em."

Before his brother could respond a low rumble echoed through the tunnels.

The people upstairs in the barn heard it too. "That's just great," Lila said. "There's nothing I'd like more than to be caught in an earthquake now. We've received news reports about underground bomb tests that set off earthquakes around the Pacific rim."

Jack told her, "I don't think what we just heard was an earthquake."

Lila put one hand to her throat. "A bomb? So close to here?"

"I don't think so."

"Well, it has to be one or the other! If it's a bomb I want to be in the shelter but if it's an earthquake I sure don't want to be underground."

Jack broke the deadlock by announcing, "It's a bomb," and began ushering the others down the steps.

In the early part of the twenty-first century an earthquake measuring eight points or more on the Richter scale occurred only once a year. Recently they had become more frequent; now they girdled the globe and their seismic roar was a warning not to be ignored. Jack had heard it before; that sound was unforgettable.

He had heard bombs too.

This was neither. It seemed more like . . .

By the time he reached the foot of the stairs the sound had stopped.

The L-shaped gallery was intended to serve as a common room. On one side a deep alcove had been fitted out as a kitchen, with a tile counter and sink, a gas stove and a cabinet for tableware. An impressive stainless-steel coffee machine had pride of place.

Otherwise the area lacked the civilized touches that made the farmhouse comfortable. The ceiling was fitted with Sheetrock, the lighting fixtures consisted of strategically placed bare bulbs in cheap paper shades. A rough cement floor was only partially covered by a couple of threadbare wool rugs. The furniture included weathered garden benches, overturned crates and a mismatched set of kitchen chairs arranged around an old pine table.

The first time Nell saw the room she had recalled the "great hall" in the Bennett house; the baronial imitation Rob Bennett had been so proud of, with its medieval chandeliers and leaded glass windows. Every piece of furniture and every accessory, no matter how small, had been chosen with the utmost care to reflect the superior status of its owner. The decorators had been forced to repaint the huge room three times before Robert Bennett was satisfied with the result.

No such effort had been expended by Edgar Tilbury. His bolt-hole was a man-shed, rough and ready.

Samson stood at the top of the stairs, gazing wistfully down at the people.

Tilbury said, "Poor bastard, he can't make it down the steps."

"Good thing he has friends," said Jack. He went up and gathered the big dog into his arms, with three legs dangling. Samson gratefully licked his face. This did not make it any easier to navigate the steps on the way down. When Jack reached the bottom he announced, "okay, everybody's here now."

He knew Mrs. Richmond was not coming; he suspected that the Fergusons weren't either. But they had to be rostered among the living for a while yet.

"I'll be happy to share the cooking with anyone who knows how to boil water," Tilbury hinted.

Bea said, "I'm famous for my boiled water. Let me help."

"Sounds good; you get kitchen duty in the morning. For tonight I'll fix supper while everyone puts their things away. Any requests?"

"How about some of your Blow-Your-Socks-Off Chili?"

"That's flattering, Lila, but remember we're going to be sharing a small space down here. I suggest something with less pow to it."

"Pow!" Flub Nyeberger exclaimed, clapping his hands together. Dub joined in a fraction of a second later.

Tilbury soon had a large pot of beef stew simmering and was cutting slices from loaves of crusty brown bread. A wheel of golden cheese waited on a wooden tray. "Any of you have a sweet tooth, you better get over it," he advised. "Dentists might be in short supply in the future." In spite of this threat he had a dessert for the children; canned pears with raisins soaked in the juice.

When the scent of cooking permeated the shelter Bea's cats appeared up one by one. The exuberant Irish setters made a nuisance of themselves, begging at the table and embarrassing Nell, but Samson just laid his big head on her thigh and gazed up at her.

Jess said, "He remembers you, Mom. He seems like a different dog now, though."

"A happier dog," her mother agreed. "He and Lila's cat are great friends, had you noticed? Rob used to brag that his dog would kill any cat he saw."

She was surprised at how easily her former husband's name came to her lips now. He had become a being from another world, receding into the distance. If she did not force herself to do it she could not recall his face.

After the meal the Nyeberger boys resumed their avid investigation of the shelter. "Don't worry about them," Nell advised Gloria. "They can't go anywhere and there's nothing down here that can hurt them. If you wonder where they are, just stop and listen. That whooping and hollering echoes a lot but it will lead you to them."

Shay took Tilbury aside. "You made your sleeping pods to hold one person. What if . . ."

"What if you and Lila want to share? If you can't solve that problem you're not the man for her," said Tilbury.

The evening passed amid brief bursts of nervous conversation and small domestic chores. Jack was distracted; he found it impossible to give his undivided attention to anything. Although he was listening as hard as he could he heard no more rumbles, no thunder of planes, no explosion of bombs. The world beyond their refuge might be perfectly peaceful.

He did not trust it.

"If any of you decide to have a look outside and see what's going on," he told the others, "take someone else with you."

Gerry replied, "I doubt if any of us wants to go alone, Jack."

"I'm just saying."

"Do you want to look outside yourself? If so, I'm up for it," Shay said.

The two men climbed the stairs and opened the side door of the barn. The air outside was very still and icy cold; sharp in the throat.

"I don't see anything, do you?"

At that moment a blue-white flash appeared in the distance, followed by another. Then another; a whole string of them. "Transformers blowing," Jack said grimly.

"Yeah, I guess we should have expected it. There goes the power."

"Not our power, unless Edgar's faith in his generator is misplaced."

"Do you think the power grid's been sabotaged?"

"I think any or everything might be sabotaged, Shay. That's the problem with being an American, we tend to believe everybody shares our Boy Scout philosophy."

"C'mon, Jack, we're not that naïve."

"On the contrary, I hope we are. If we ever lose that cock-eyed optimism we'll be as bad as the enemy."

They gazed into the dark, each man alone with his thoughts. Then together they returned to warmth and light.


Tilbury's bomb shelter was like being at summer camp, Jack decided as he crawled into his sleeping pod. You could put up with the inconveniences if you knew you'd be going home at the end of the season.

But there had to be a definable end and a familiar world waiting.

He spent the night trying to accommodate his tall body to the size and shape of the pod, unable to fall asleep and not ready to be awake.

In the morning he had the headache that had been haunting him for days.

Bea's breakfast consisted of poached eggs with a slice of cheese topping whole-grain wheat toast, and strips of bacon fried to perfection. Tilbury made a big show of gazing into his empty cup and lamenting, "Where's my boiled water?"

As she gave him his cup Bea said, "Here; I poured it through a brown sock."

The coffee was perfect too, prepared in the best coffee-maker Bea had ever seen.

After their meal those who possessed working AllComs pooled them in hope of extracting a comprehensible message from the frequent static. Tilbury's homemade device was the most successful; at times a whole sentence or two was transmitted. "Please contact the emergency services on this number and be sure to give your access and zip codes." "The entire area between Claypool and Nolan's Falls may be contaminated. Go to the general hospital at Merrymount for treatment."

"Contaminated with what? Are they using chemical warfare?"

No one could answer the question.

Tilbury had taken the precaution of equipping his property with a sensitive alarm system that worked on sound vibrations and warned him of any visitors. The system was connected to the house, the barn, and the cattle guard at the end of the lane. Whenever he entered the tunnels it was turned on.

The cattle guard was his first line of defense.

When its shrill whistle sounded Tilbury went hurrying toward the stairs. Jack intercepted him.

"We've got company, Jack; I'm going up to meet them."

"Not without me, you're not."

"Didn't I show you this? Look here."

Tucked under the stairs was a small telescreen that revealed a sedan now driving toward the house. Tilbury said thankfully, "It's the Fergusons."

"You know their car by sight?"

"I . . . well, not exactly, but who else would it be?"

"I'll go with you," Jack said firmly. "And don't open your door to them until you're sure who you're letting in. I know from spending time in the Mideast: a dangerous desperation can take hold when war breaks out. Nice people turn into strangers."

# 17

The barn stood on a hill near the back of the property. The site had excellent drainage; the building had been set at an angle that prevented anyone at the front of the house from seeing it.

Tilbury was fond of saying, "If you didn't know it was there you'd never know it was there."

Jack and Tilbury walked briskly to the house, entered through the kitchen door, made their way to the living room and peered through the heavy lace curtains. Three adults were standing on the front porch. "Are those your friends, Edgar?" Jack asked in a low voice.

"It's Bob and Mildred, all right; I don't see their girls. I don't know the man who's with them."

"Did they say anything about bringing another person?"

"No, and that's kind of odd."

"You bet it is. Would you take a stranger to an invitation-only bomb shelter?"

"I told you, Jack, I've known Bob for years. If he vouches for that guy with him—"

"*I* haven't heard him vouch for anyone. Wait here and keep quiet."

"What are you—"

"I said wait and be quiet. If they're on the up-and-up it'll be fine. And don't worry, I won't embarrass you."

As silently as smoke, Jack left the room.

This was a side of him Tilbury had never seen.

The stranger with Bob Ferguson stabbed the doorbell with an impatient forefinger. Ferguson said something to him; he gave a negative shake of his head and hit the doorbell again.

"Hey, Bob!" called a cheery voice. Jack Reece appeared at the foot of the porch steps and came up to them in a single bound. "And the missus too, that's great. We've been waiting for you." Before Ferguson could think of a response Jack held out his hand to the stranger and said, "Jack Reece, I'm the local chief of police and an old pal of Bob's, I'm sure he's mentioned me."

Mildred Ferguson, white faced, was standing rigidly beside her husband.

The stranger glowered at Jack. "Police?"

"Why sure. Isn't it funny how often I get that? I must look like a movie star or something. Here . . ." Jack slid his fingers into a jacket pocket and removed a brown leather wallet. Another smooth gesture flipped the wallet open to reveal what looked like a badge, which he thrust in the other man's face briefly before closing the wallet and returning it to his pocket.

"We're having a meeting of the local constabulary here today," he went on in a jovial tone, "and Bob's going to do some contract work for us." He looked at Ferguson. "Did you bring those specs along?"

Bob Ferguson was almost as quick a thinker as Jack Reece. "With all hell breaking loose I wasn't sure—"

"We'd go ahead with the deal? Sure we will; business is business, that's what capitalism is all about, eh?" Jack gave the stranger a shove in the ribs that lingered a little too long. "First though, come inside and meet the rest of the bunch, they're eager to—"

"I have to go," the stranger told Ferguson. "Give me your facial plate."

Ferguson dug in his pocket and took out the small metal rectangle that identified his features. The man snatched it out of his hand and sprinted for the sedan.

"Stop him!" Mildred Ferguson pleaded. She turned wild eyes on Jack. "They have our girls!"

"And he's got enough weapons on him to kill us all," Jack said grimly.

Edgar Tilbury came out onto the porch to watch the stranger speed away in the Fergusons' car. "What in hell's this about, Bob? And where are your girls?"

Mildred Ferguson gave a heartbroken sob and slumped against the porch railing. A top-heavy woman with thin legs, she unaccountably had chosen a silk print dress and sheer nylons to wear to a bomb shelter.

Her husband was a heavyset man with a chapped complexion and gaps between his front teeth. "I got a late start, Ed;

sorry about that. Yesterday was one of those days when everything went wrong, but we left the house first thing this morning. Bombs had been dropped on Claypool and civil defense warned they might be chemical warfare, so I took the shortcut from the interstate where it angles through that big stretch of woods. We saw another car pulled over on the side of the road like it'd broken down. The driver waved to me and I stopped to see if I could help. You'd do the same."

"I wouldn't," Jack said coldly.

Ferguson glanced at him, then back to Tilbury. "The man pulled a gun on me and demanded my car."

"Looters," Jack said with disgust. "It doesn't take long for the bottom feeders to crawl out from under their rocks."

"I wasn't expecting . . . anyway, he looked in the backseat and saw the girls and gave a shout. Another man came out of the trees. He had a gun too. He held it on Mildred while the first shithead took . . . took my girls into the woods and . . ."

"Don't," said Edgar.

"My wife couldn't keep her big mouth shut," Ferguson continued bitterly. "She had to tell them about your bomb shelter."

"If I offered something of value in return I thought maybe they'd let the girls go."

"They didn't, did they?"

"I'm sorry—"

"If you say that one more time I'll—"

"Don't," Jack echoed Tilbury. "Just tell us what happened next."

"One man stayed with the girls while the other one came with us to see if there really was a safe shelter."

"He may have intended to shoot you both and double-cross his partner by taking the shelter for himself," Jack said. "I don't suppose he knew how big it was or how many other people would be here?"

"Mildred only told him it was safe. That's what everyone's looking for, even crooks. But what am I going to do now? He's got my car and my girls are . . ."

"If you had a car would you try to rescue them?"

"Damn straight I would!" Bob Ferguson cried.

Jack said, "I'm sorry to be brutal, but here are the facts. Your girls are likely dead by now."

Mildred Ferguson stared at him as if he were a monster.

"Those thugs you met are the kind that travel light," he told her. "They wouldn't want living witnesses. If your husband blunders onto the scene again you'll be a widow. You don't have any option; come into the shelter now. When it's possible, if it ever is possible, I'll help you look for your girls."

Ferguson said, "Who the fuck is this guy, Ed?"

"Someone who's giving you good advice."

"Is he the chief of police, like he said?"

Tilbury tugged at his earlobe. "I'd say Jack's whoever he wants to be."

Although he was shaken, Bob Ferguson managed to walk to the barn and go down the stairs, but his wife was unable to walk. Shay Mulligan diagnosed severe shock; he and the Delmonicos improvised a stretcher for her.

"I don't have a sedative for a human," Shay said. "A lot of veterinary medicine crosses the boundaries but I wouldn't want to take the chance. Edgar, why didn't you include a GP in your circle of friends?"

"Didn't think of it; I never go to the doctor."

"Yet you brought a first aid kit and a defibrillator."

"I didn't anticipate anything like this."

Jack snorted. "From now on everything that happens will be something we didn't anticipate."

Tucking Mildred Ferguson into a sleeping pod was out of the question; a bed was prepared for her in one of the tunnels and Tilbury gave the distraught woman enough Irish whiskey to "put her out of her misery for the rest of the day." Gloria sat with her until she was asleep, then returned to the others. "The poor woman's almost out of her mind with grief," she reported. "I don't know how we're going to manage when she comes around."

"Knock her in the head, for all I care," said her husband.

"You don't mean that."

"You think not? Listen, I've been married to that waste of space for seventeen years and I know her. Opera singer. Artistic temperament and all that. Big deal. This is entirely her fault."

"You're one of those people who blames everyone but himself," Jack told Ferguson. "Edgar thought enough of you to include you in his shelter, but I suspect he made a mistake. Maybe you belong outside."

Ferguson blinked. "You wouldn't do that."

"Try me." Jack's voice was low and very soft.

"Edgar?" Ferguson appealed to him.

Tilbury was not a people person. The shelter and its design were his idea, but he had never considered the organization of the society within it. He was a practical man, however. Jack Reece he recognized as a natural leader. Under the circumstances he would be worth more than a business acquaintance. "If Jack wants to put you out . . ." Tilbury left the sentence unfinished.

Bob Ferguson had just seen Jack Reece in action. He sank onto one of the kitchen chairs. "I'm grateful, Ed, really I am, and I'm sure Mildred is too. We're just . . . our girls . . ." He sagged as if all the air had gone out of his lungs.

Jack asked, "Is it true about chemical warfare?"

"Hard to tell," Ferguson replied in a leaden voice. "The folks at civil defense seemed to think so; I guess we won't know for sure until people start dropping dead."

"We won't see that down here," Tilbury assured him. "I've installed a stringent air filtration system."

"Will it handle radioactive particles?"

"Are they dropping atom bombs yet?" Gerry wanted to know.

Tilbury said, "Ask Lila; she's monitoring communications, such as they are."

"A missile with a nuclear warhead was reported striking the northwest coast this morning," Lila responded, "but it hasn't been confirmed. That's all I've heard so far. The news is sporadic at best. If we were on the surface we might get better reception but no one wants to be on the surface."

"Amen," said Bea Fontaine.

The lights flickered briefly. They all tensed.

"Where the hell's your generator, Edgar?"

"It just cut in, can't you tell? There's a slight difference in brightness."

"So something's affected the power grid?"

"Apparently."

Evan Mulligan said, "I didn't think it would happen this fast."

"Of course you didn't. War is for the history books, but who teaches history these days?"

"When I was in high school we could take a history course for extra credit," Evan said, "but I don't know anyone who did. I mean, it wouldn't prepare you for a good job."

"No," Tilbury agreed. "A knowledge of history only prepares you for life. Here's an example. In the twentieth century—which was not the Dark Ages, no matter what you may think—there was a madman named Adolf Hitler. He was full of grand ideas and extravagant plans and he promised to make Germany great again.

"Adolf Hitler talked a good game. He told people exactly what they wanted to hear, so they believed him. He never let a little thing like the truth stand in his way. He climbed through the political ranks with a combination of overheated oratory, bluster and bravado. When members of the established government disagreed with him they were replaced by his own cronies; handpicked henchmen who constantly lavished praise on him. He couldn't get enough of it. He surrounded himself with the most scurrilous pack of yes-men ever born, and they encouraged him to do whatever he wanted.

"The law couldn't stop him; he simply issued new laws.

"Hitler's followers were known as Nazis, and within a few years the Nazi hierarchy were living in mansions and hunting stags in the Black Forest. They stole famous works of art and collected beautiful women. Anything they wanted was theirs for the taking.

"Ordinary people were too scared to stand up to the Nazis; they might get a knock on their door late at night. If they had the wrong name or the wrong blood in their veins they could be sent to a concentration camp. Most of those never came back."

Jess pleated her smooth forehead into a frown. "The Germans must have been really stupid to let the Nazis get away with anything like that."

"On the contrary, the Germans were among the best educated people in Europe."

"Are you sure about that, Edgar? It sounds, like, preposterous."

"Even intelligent people will accept the preposterous if it's coated with sugar and fed to them a bite at a time."

Jess was unconvinced. "Not me!"

Tilbury smiled knowingly. "Hitler became more and more arrogant. Everything the man said was the truth—because he said it was. He claimed he was creating 'The Thousand Year Reich,' and a lot of people believed him.

"Once Germany had been highly regarded for its scholarship and culture, but under Hitler it became the enemy of all that was decent. He didn't care. All he cared about was himself. The Thousand Year Reich didn't last for a decade, but that was long enough for Hitler and his Nazis to exterminate millions by the most cruel methods possible. He particularly hated the Jews. He ordered the murder of people who might have made a great contribution to society: scientists, artists, intellectuals; youngsters whose lives of promise were cut short; men and women who could think for themselves and not follow along like lambs to the slaughter."

The lights flickered again.

Mildred Ferguson's shrill scream echoed through the shelter. "My little girls!"

# 18

By the time Gloria and Nell reached her, Kirby was already there. He was sitting beside Mildred and stroking her hand while he murmured in a soothing monotone. He looked up at the two women. "She came to in the dark, and was really scared. I know all about really scared. Do you think Edgar could bring more light in here for her?"

"My little girls. My little girls." Repeated like a mantra.

"We need to take her to a hospital," Gloria told Nell. "This is the worst possible situation for her; she's frightened out of her mind."

"Would more whiskey—"

"I'd be afraid to try; I don't know what her tolerance is and she might get alcohol poisoning. Besides, she's so distressed she'd probably keep throwing it off."

"My little girls . . ." The mantra was fading but relentless.

"I was so relieved when we got here," said Gloria. "I knew we weren't really *safe,* but we were much better off. This poor woman isn't."

"Everything's relative. Suppose those men had raped her too and left her dead in the woods?"

"She might prefer it," Gloria said sadly. "Who knows what we're facing now?"

"The only way out is through."

"Where'd you hear that, Nell?"

"Jack says it sometimes; I'm beginning to understand what he means."

Kirby interjected, "My plastic surgeon says it too."

Gloria wanted to wrap her arms around him. "You poor dear, when will you get the rest of your surgery?"

He recalled the way Jess Bennett had smiled at him. "Even if I don't, I'll be all right. Being alive is what counts. The rest is like the piles of stuff we brought with us. Here, Gloria, you stroke her hand the way I'm doing and I'll go talk to Edgar about the lighting. Be back in a minute."

When Kirby had gone Nell said, "How wrong can anyone be? I used to wonder why you took those children."

Gloria shrugged. "It was something I had to do."

"Are you always so impulsive?"

"I suppose I am. Gerry says I keep surprising him."

"I'll bet you do . . . perhaps Jack would like for me to surprise him sometimes."

"He loves you the way you are, Nell."

"Does he? Miss Prim and Proper? That's how others think of me, I suppose, but inside I'm—"

"Come quick, both of you!" Kirby shouted. "You have to see this!"

When the two women entered the common room they stopped abruptly. The space was flooded with a pale violet light; almost opalescent.

"Isn't that beautiful," Gloria murmured. "How did you do it, Edgar?"

"I didn't. It just appeared."

"An unusual light like that doesn't appear on its own."

"This one did."

Jack said, "We were talking when the electricity flickered again, then Kirby came in wanting a glass of water for Mildred Ferguson. Next thing we knew the lights went out completely and . . . now I know where I saw it before!"

"There was a similar light in the parking lot," Nell reminded him.

"This was long before then; a dozen years ago. I was in Indonesia touring the Ring of Fire with a couple of friends of mine. We wanted to climb the notorious Mount Merapi—the name means 'Fire Mountain'—but were warned it might erupt at any time. We went anyway. We'd just reached the summit when we heard the most godawful roar. I looked down into the crater and glimpsed that same light in its heart. We fell over each other getting off the mountain."

"And did it erupt?"

"Not then, but I felt like I'd been warned. I didn't go back."

Bea said reprovingly, "You never told me that story."

"There are a lot of things I don't tell you, Aunt Bea."

As Jack spoke the violet light dimmed, bleeding into the

shadows in the corners of the room. Within seconds the electric lights came back on.

"We all need a cup of coffee after that," Bea said. She went into the alcove but came back out again, looking puzzled. "What happened to your coffee machine, Edgar?"

"Nothing better happen to that machine," he growled as he hurried to see. "What the . . . those little motherfuckers! Wait till I get my hands on them!"

"The boys didn't do this, Edgar." Bea indicated the featureless silvery pile on the tile counter. "I came in here a few minutes ago to get a drink of water and your machine was fine then. The twins and Buster were off exploring, and Kirby was with your friend's wife, so they're innocent."

"No coffee," Tilbury moaned. "Just when you think things can't get any worse."

"There's a jar of instant in the back of the cabinet."

"That *would* make things worse."

The others crowded in to examine the ruined machine. Jack ran a finger over the surface. Cold. Slightly grainy and not quite hard. "Stainless steel's an alloy but what else is in it, Edgar?"

"Chromium and nickel, if memory serves, and—"

"Shut up about your fucking coffeemaker!" Bob Ferguson bellowed. "Who cares? My wife's lost her marbles and my daughters are missing and you promised to help me find them! So why aren't you doing something? What kind of people are you, anyway?"

"Scared people, just like you," said Lila Ragland. "We're down here hoping to save our lives because we think war's broken out, but we're not sure. Until we know what's happening it would be stupid to go outside."

"Well, I'm going, and the rest of you can stay here and rot!" He bolted for the stairs.

"Oh, for God's sake." Jack dived after him.

"Let him go!" called Shay. "We can't keep him here if he doesn't want to stay."

Jack almost caught Ferguson. He was only a few steps behind when the other man slammed the trapdoor on him, forcefully striking the top of his head.


"Not having a doctor in this group is the worst mistake you ever made, Edgar," Nell said angrily. She was sitting cross-legged on the floor, holding Jack's head on her lap. He was bleeding onto a folded towel while Shay Mulligan tried to staunch the flow and Bea Fontaine hovered anxiously over them. The veterinarian was not offended by Nell's remark, even though he had a stethoscope around his neck and a medical bag open beside him.

Jack's eyes were closed. His face was bleached of color.

"If I knew where to find a doctor I'd go get him," said Tilbury, "but I never use them." He added, "I personally believe they killed Veronica."

"What about your neighbors, don't they—"

"My nearest neighbors live more than a mile from here and we're barely on speaking terms. Little dispute over property lines."

"We need to know what's going on outside," Shay insisted.

The words were hardly out of his mouth when they heard an explosion. "That sounds like your house got bombed, Edgar."

"I don't think so, it was too far away."

"Maybe it hit your neighbors, then."

"Could be. From the sound at least it was a conventional bomb."

"Thank the Lord for small favors," said Bea.

A second explosion followed the first. Within a few seconds there was a third, but the sounds were decreasing in volume. "The bombers are flying north," Tilbury guessed.

The first explosion had been enough to send everyone running to the common room, adults and children alike. Even the Nyeberger twins were subdued as the group clustered around Jack and Nell.

Gerry said, "You still want to go outside, Shay?"

Without looking up, he pressed a fresh pad of cotton to Jack's head. "My patient needs me here."

"We all need you here," Lila told him.

No one was more aware of this than Edgar Tilbury. In a situation where a leader was imperative, the obvious choice had been sidelined. The mantle might fall on him. He didn't even like people, though his eccentric pastime had made it possible for him to save a number of lives. He recognized the irony. Tilbury was a lifelong atheist; someone like Gloria Delmonico might have seen the hand of providence at work.

While the echoes of the bombing died away the group in the shelter waited. Even the animals were quiet, though some of them cast questioning looks at their two-legged gods.

"What now?" Bea said at last.

No one had an answer.

Fear has a short shelf life. Abject terror can fuel it for longer, but the repetition of daily routine eventually has a soothing effect. While they waited the inhabitants of the shelter washed and brushed and ate and defecated. The adults talked, the children played, the animals organized their own societies. The dogs had one, the cats another. Only Samson was welcome in both.

Shay and Gloria became an ad hoc medical team, caring for Jack as well as for Mildred Ferguson.

Gloria was sanguine about Jack's condition. "Head wounds bleed a lot," she explained to Nell, "but he has a good strong pulse. He'll come around soon. That heavy door gave him quite a blow but I don't think there's any permanent damage done."

"If there is, I hope they drop one of those bombs on Bob Ferguson."

"You don't mean that."

"I certainly do! Now I know why soldiers feel murderous on the battlefield."

Gloria said reasonably, "For most of them it's only a job."

Nell wasn't open to reason at the moment. "I can't imagine my son, Colin, as a soldier, thinking what he did was 'a job.' How callous is that?"

Kirby was spending much of his time with Mildred Ferguson. When he held her hand she relaxed, which was gratifying. If she was awake she looked at the ceiling instead of his face, which was a relief. Sometimes she talked to her daughters as if they were beside her.

Kirby knew what being damaged meant. He asked Gloria, "Is Mrs. Ferguson's damage temporary?"

"It doesn't have to be. If we could take her to a hospital like Staunton Memorial and give her proper medication in addition to therapy, in a few weeks you'd see a great improvement."

"What if she doesn't get the medication?"

"She might recover on her own."

"*I* won't," Kirby said sadly.

Warned by the incident of the coffeemaker, Tilbury made a dozen trips a day to the end of the tunnel where the machinery had been installed; each time he examined the generator as thoroughly as if he had never seen one before.

Anxiety was contagious; soon everyone was on guard. The Nyeberger twins, whose interest had always been in destruction, became advocates for protection. They checked belt buckles and metal cutlery as if their lives depended on it.

No other metal failed.

"It's crazy," Gerry said flatly. "Whatever destroyed the coffeemaker must still be in here, but where is it?"

Bedtime came early in the shelter. Aside from making use of Tilbury's library there was not much to do. They could not see the darkness descending outside, yet people sensed it. The animals continued to be diurnal. The AllComs had become unreliable, but there was no shortage of battery-run clocks, yet no one consulted them; time seemed to have a different span underground.

The atmosphere in the common room was claustrophobic; in the sleeping pods it was worse. Tilbury only used his because the cats avoided them. The kids thought the pods were great fun, but after a night or two the other adults took their bedding into the common room and slept there, most of them in their clothes. They felt less vulnerable when they were dressed.

"Remember how the Wednesday Club wanted to be together after the bomb in the Baltic?" Bea remarked as she snuggled under her blanket. "We're like a tribe."

"So are they," said Gerry Delmonico as Bea's cats took their accustomed positions around her. Driving the horse-bus had made him more sensitive to the interaction between people and animals.

When he believed everyone was asleep Shay Mulligan quietly made his way up the stairs with a flashlight in one hand.

A strong push raised the trapdoor; he eased through and let it down again without making any noise.

There was only one bicycle leaning against the wall. The angle was so acute Shay thought the machine might fall over. With his free hand he took hold of the handlebars to straighten it up.

The metal was grainy; not quite hard.

When Shay pushed the bicycle back against the wall the frame slumped as if it were tired.

With a sinking heart he noticed the side door was slightly ajar. Shay ran to the door and flung it open, but Bob Ferguson and the other bicycle had long since disappeared.

How far would he get before the machine failed?

As Shay turned around, the beam from his flashlight fell on Jack Reece's car, parked just inside the big front doors.

He trotted across the barn floor to the blue coupé. It looked the same as always but he needed to touch it to be sure—and he didn't want to find out. If the car could not be driven . . .

Clenching his jaw, he laid his hand on the hood.

"How is it?" asked a voice from the shadows.

Shay gave a start. "Edgar! I didn't see you over there."

"I followed you to see what you're doing."

"I tried not to disturb anyone."

"We're all what you might call disturbed tonight. And I got ears like a rat, I heard you when you put your foot on the first step. So answer my question; how's the car? Has it collapsed like that bicycle over there?"

"Come over here and see for yourself."

Shay stepped back.

Tilbury put his hand palm down on the hood. A quizzical expression spread over his face. "What the holy hell is that?"

"You feel it too?"

"Damned right I do! It's almost like flesh. Not human flesh; a fish's, maybe. But I can't—what the devil's happening now!" Tilbury stepped away from the car and held up his hand.

His fingers were glowing with a violet light.

He sat down hard on the nearest bale of hay. As the glow faded he released a stream of highly original profanities.

Shay said, "I'm impressed, Edgar; I didn't know you had it in you."

"Neither did I. Touch that car again, will you?"

"After what it did to you?"

"Don't worry, it won't bite. Just touch it."

Shay ran his fingertips across the hood, then presented them for Tilbury's inspection. There was no violet light, but a faint indentation remained in the metal. "No one's going to drive this car again, Edgar."

"And I'll never have another decent cup of coffee," the other man said sourly. "Wish I knew who to blame. Jack has a theory that someone on the other side's using a new kind of weapon, an electromagnetic pulse that's designed to disrupt the atoms in metal alloys. A thing like that could do terrible damage to human beings; it'd go right through them."

"Is it possible?"

"You're an animal doctor; surely you're aware that years ago medical science discovered old-fashioned cell phones could destroy brain tissue."

"I read that in school; it would support Jack's theory."

"Except there's a couple of holes in it," Tilbury said. "How do you explain the random nature of the destruction? Or its slow progression, for that matter? The thing that ruins metal strikes here, strikes there; sometimes large objects and sometimes little ones. There's simply no pattern to the son of a bitch. Surely a weapon intended to be catastrophic would unleash one mighty blast, it wouldn't destroy inch by inch. That's a different technique.

"When I was a teenager in New England we suffered from a plague of gypsy moths every year. They'd work their way north, stripping the leaves from the trees as they came. They could devastate a whole forest of hardwood or sugar maples in a few days, killing all the trees and costing the owners a fortune. Those little bastards did it inch by inch. Finally someone discovered an insecticide that destroyed the moth eggs before they hatched, and eventually that took care of it. But for several years I made pocket money hunting through the woods, searching for those eggs."

Shay sat down on the bale beside Tilbury. "We aren't

being attacked by some bug, Edgar. We can't solve our problem that easily."

"Easily? It was bloody hard work, I'll tell you. One time I got chased up a tree by a black bear."

Shay laughed.

Tilbury didn't. "I guarantee there's not a scientist in America who knows how to solve this. They didn't know how to stop the Change either, but after a while we adapted to it."

"And then it stopped of its own accord."

"And then it stopped," Tilbury agreed, "but of its own accord? We don't have any idea what was behind the Change, but I'd be willing to bet everything I have that *something* was behind it. And that something's coming at us again."

# 19

"What's coming at us," Shay said, "is war. Everything in me rebels against hiding underground at the mercy of events I have no control over. I came up here, Edgar, to—"

"To thumb your nose at the war?"

"It sounds silly when you put it like that. Say I'm suffering from claustrophobia."

"Are you planning on going outside? *That* would be silly; it would amount to throwing away the chance of life I've given you."

"And that sounds pretentious. Come on, Edgar; you didn't even know me when you started digging those tunnels down there. Why'd you do it, anyway? That's a hell of an expensive hobby."

Tilbury tugged at his earlobe. "Maybe I was showing off for Veronica."

"Your wife? Didn't she die years ago?"

"She did. But I still show off for her."

"You must have loved her very much."

"I do. Do love her very much."

"Present tense?"

"Because she's here."

"Her spirit is, you mean."

"No; Veronica's buried in this hill. The law said I had to put her in the cemetery with a lot of strangers and leave her there, so I did, but every week I drove to Sycamore River to visit her grave. Those trips kept reminding me how much distance there was between us. So finally I paid Bob Ferguson to help sneak her out of Sunnyslope and bring her here."

Shay could not think of anything to say.

An explosion sounded in the distance. One of the carriage horses lashed out in its stall. Thunder of hooves against wooden planks.

Tilbury got up and walked stiffly to the big double doors. "Damned arthritis." He slid open one of the doors far enough to peer out.

"What do you see?" Shay called.

"The back of my house and that's about it. You have to go three miles up the main road to get a good look at anything but hills and trees. At least there's been no nuclear explosion; we'd be able to see that in the night sky." Tilbury returned to the hay bale and grunted with effort as he sat down. "Sounds like they're bombing the airfield at Nolan's Falls now."

"Do you suppose Bob Ferguson got that far?"

"I doubt it, Shay; not on that bicycle. But you have to give him credit for trying."

"I give him credit for abandoning his wife in a fit of temper and maybe getting himself killed."

"You wouldn't go looking for those girls, Don Quixote?"

Shay considered the question. "Jack would if he weren't injured."

"Yeah, but he's a major risk taker."

"How can you tell? Have you seen him in action?"

"I've seen him enter a room," Tilbury said. "The first thing he does is look around for the nearest exit. Once he's got that located, he always sits down with his back to the wall."

"That's it?"

"That's all the information I need."

"You have your wires crossed. It sounds like Jack's cautious, which is the reverse of a risk taker."

"Those habits are the result of experience. Put them together with a dozen others I've observed and they're a dead giveaway. Jack likes life at the edge; he may not be around for much longer."

"You could say that about any of us under the circumstances."

"I've had most of my life already, so I'm not complaining. But you . . . let me give you a word of advice, Shay. Lila Ragland's a major risk taker too."

"Why do you say that?"

"It's based on everything I know about her, and I suspect there's a lot of it you don't know."

"You wouldn't be trying to discourage me, would you?"

"No, because you seem to be making Lila happy, and that's good enough for me. But when we come out of this, if we come out of this, we may be different people. We could be in here for a long time with no one to talk to but one another. That sounds like a small thing but it's not.

"Before the Change most communication took place through the electronic media. We were living with total connectivity yet people had never been so far apart. But as their emails and social media began failing they had to talk to each other face-to-face. It was a steep learning curve for a lot of them"—Tilbury chuckled—"but they ran out of options just in time to save the art of conversation. What a loss that would have been! I even had a bumper sticker made: DISCONNECT YOUR DEVICES. RECONNECT WITH PEOPLE."

"I bought one of those!" Shay exclaimed.

"Did you do what it said?"

"Well . . . no. The concept sounded good but everyone used email, it was . . ."

"Addictive. Yeah. We humans are mighty stubborn, Shay. Learning—I don't mean education, that's someone else's learning regurgitated—has to be forced on us. If we stay in the shelter for very long you're going to learn a lot of things about the folks in here with you. Some of it may be stuff you didn't want to know."

Another explosion sounded, near enough to make the two men flinch.

"That's another form of communication," Shay remarked.

"Yeah, with a meaning we can't misunderstand. For decades we've endured regional skirmishes instead of all-out war, with each side threatening to nuke the other out of existence. This had to happen sooner or later."

"The nuke part too?"

"Definitely the nuke part, we're too stupid to avoid it. Come on, let's go down below."

Shay got to his feet. "Not me; I have to *know*. Stay there and keep things working in the shelter, Edgar. I'm going to saddle a horse."

Major risk taker, Shay thought to himself as he walked across the barn, weaving around the farm machinery.

Some of it was slumping.

Shay knew his concentration should be on the situation ahead but his mind seemed to have veered onto a byway. Was Edgar trying to warn him of something? Jack and Lila are major risk takers; does he mean that like attracts like?

He heard the thump as Edgar threw back the trapdoor. Turning around, Shay called, "Did you say three miles up the main road?"

"More or less. Shouldn't take you long on a horse. As soon as you get a good look, scurry home, will you? If you meet Bob Ferguson on the way drag him back by the scruff of his neck. I have a few choice words to say to that man."

The trapdoor banged shut.

A snaffle bridle and two saddles hung on pegs outside Rocket's stall. Since acquiring the cart Evan did not ride the chestnut mare often; the western saddle had a thin coating of dust on it. The stirrups of the English saddle would need adjusting. Evan's taller than I am now, Shay mused as he shortened the leathers.

Inside her stall, Rocket pricked her ears with interest.

"You ready for a little exercise?" he asked.

Her answer was a soft nicker.

When the horse was tacked up Shay led her from the barn. One of the carriage horses whinnied to them as they passed.

"Not this time, old fellow. I may need someone who can run."

Shay led the mare as far as the cattle guard, then guided her carefully across the suspended iron rails before mounting. It felt good to be in a saddle again.

I should ride more often, he told himself, but I never have the time.

On the main road they broke into a brisk trot. The horse had better night vision than the man, but in spite of his sense of urgency Shay did not let her gallop. Not a major risk taker.

He knew how long it would take to ride three miles. He was almost there when he heard a banshee wail of warning. The eerie voice of sirens rose and fell, rose and fell. Shay shortened the reins, trying to decide what to do. Turn around, go on . . . he tightened his legs on the mare's sides just as the earth heaved upward, reacting to the massive concussion that hammered Nolan's Falls and spread outward in concentric circles.

Rocket shied violently.

Shay was a good rider but he was unready. He sailed through the air and landed flat on his back on the hard road.

Erasmus Barber had an organized mind. He liked to picture the inside of his head as an old-fashioned rolltop desk with an assigned space for everything. Envelopes in this cubbyhole and stationery in that one, insurance policies in a top drawer, receipts organized by date, wills in the locked compartment in the middle. The arrangement made him feel good; in control.

War was one thing he could not control. This one had erupted while he was trying to decide whether to invest in a bomb shelter or move out of the country. When the bomb hit Nolan's Falls he and his wife were just leaving town, driving back to Benning. On her lap Maybelline held a large folder of sales material about bomb shelters; she wanted to buy one and have it installed in their backyard.

In spite of the salesman's spiel Erasmus was unconvinced. He had not married her for her brains. His wife must look up to him, not down on him.

"If you read those carefully, Sweetie," he pointed out, "you won't find any guarantee they can fully protect us in case of an atom bomb."

"Well, they couldn't *guarantee* that, could they? But it's been thirty years since all those tests in the Pacific and you heard what the salesman said, our side's come up with lots of new technology since then. If we get their top-of-the-line . . . what was that? Razz? What was that noise? *Stop the car!*"

Barber slammed on the brakes. They both jumped out, staring back toward the town they had just left.

The glossy sales brochures with their comforting promises slid from her lap and onto the road.

An unearthly light swelled across the sky and enveloped them. Barber reached out to grab his wife's hand just as her hair flamed. Before he could react to her shrill scream he felt a prickling sensation throughout his body, as if gravity were being canceled.

Then he was gone.

In a fraction of an instant Erasmus and Maybelline Barber became minuscule components of an incandescent gas.

Nolan's Falls smoked, steamed, vanished in a ball of light. The flimsy structures of mankind were bashed and buffeted, houses collapsed on their inhabitants, bark burned off trees, paving in the streets melted. Glass shattered into a million deadly shards.

It took less time than the blink of an eye for a pleasant town and a comfortable way of life to vanish from the earth.

# 20

Lila saw Tilbury coming down the stairs. "Is Shay up there?"

"Not now, I imagine he's on his way."

Her heart began to pound. "On his way where? Don't tell me he's gone outside!"

"Cabin fever was getting to him, I guess. That, and wanting to know about the bombing."

"The only thing we need to know is whether or not it's conventional warfare. Is it just war or has all hell broken loose?"

"Lila, *all* war is hell broken loose."

"So where's Shay gone?"

"He saddled one of the horses to ride down the main road a bit; he'll be back soon."

Lila brushed past Tilbury and took the stairs two at a time.


Jack Reece awoke with a terrible headache, but not the one that had been haunting him. This time the pain radiated from the top of his head. When he put his hand up he could feel a thick pad of cotton and gauze taped over his injury.

He sat up in increments, waiting for the dizziness to abate. "Hello?"

"I'm here!" Gloria called. She stepped into his range of vision. "You're back with us, that's good news."

"What the hell happened to me?"

"Bob Ferguson dropped the trapdoor on your head."

"I don't remember."

"I'm not surprised. At first we thought he might have fractured your skull."

Jack gave her a lopsided smile. "My head's too hard for that, but I do seem to have double vision. Was I knocked out for long?"

Gloria looked down at the diamond watch on her slim brown wrist. "You slept around the clock a couple of times; we were getting worried about you. Obviously sleep was what you needed but I'm relieved to see you're awake and rational now. You may have had a concussion; without proper medical facilities I can't be sure. Double vision's one of the symptoms. It should clear up on its own if you don't push it. In the meantime I'm going to give you a couple of Edgar's aspirins with a glass of water, and by morning you should feel better."

"I feel a little nauseated right now."

"That's another of the symptoms."

Bea Fontaine was hovering around the bed. "Is he going to be all right?"

"Your nephew's as tough as old boots. He'll die of old age at a hundred and fifty."

"In the Mars colony," Jack interjected.

Bea continued to talk over his head. "This isn't the first concussion he's had, you know; he was such a daredevil as a boy. He was always climbing trees and going up on the roof, and then he got a motorbike . . . he was supposed to wear a helmet but I used to find it under his bed."

Jack told Gloria, "You should take off that metal watch and put it in your pocket."

"If it disintegrates on my arm will it hurt me?"

"I don't know, but don't take the chance. Now tell me what happened while I was unconscious."

"Not much," she lied. "Nothing you need to worry about."

In the days when he rode show jumpers Shay Mulligan had learned how to fall. The experience saved him now. Before his body hit the ground he lifted his head just enough to keep it from striking the pavement.

The fall knocked the breath out of him. He lay supine, eyes closed, gasping for air, aware that when he moved it was going to hurt.

He would have to move sooner or later.

*I shouldn't have brought Rocket. If she's injured Evan will never forgive me.*

Shay opened his eyes.

There was a hideous glow in the sky.

*That's it.*

All the questions were answered.

Indifferent to pain now, Shay propped himself on one elbow and looked toward the north.

The intensity of the light was so great it blotted out everything but itself and its rapidly expanding dimensions, which turned night to day. The light painted the hills blue-white, the living trees blue-white, the innocent countryside blue-white, a stark arena in which a mighty pillar of smoke was rising up and up and . . .

Miles away, Shay thought with the small part of his dazed mind that was functioning. "It's miles away."

Fire bloomed with a deadly beauty inside the pillar of smoke. Behind its veil, evil eyes of red and gold gazed outward in triumph. The flames were being fed by the homes and schools and offices of Nolan's Falls; the men and women and children who had felt safe there, going to work, studying, preparing for Christmas, dreaming their dreams of a better life.

In the future.

That would never come.

People of flesh and blood and spirit had vanished into the omnipotent, deadly mushroom of man's own making.

"God," said Shay Mulligan as he lay in the road. He was not trying to express his emotions or communicate with his creator. His emotions were stunned. There could be no communication with the terrible light.

Trying to shut out the sight he would see for the rest of his life, Shay buried his face in the crook of his arm. He wanted to cry but there were no tears in his eyes. The light had burned them dry.

The bomb had exploded miles away, yet already its force was being felt in the countryside. Unrecognizable dark, smoldering bits that had once been part of something larger were beginning to rain from the sky in a torrent of gray ash.

Some of that ash had once been human.

When Shay felt the velvety touch on the back of his neck he concentrated all his thoughts on it, clinging to the comfort he needed.

Rocket nuzzled him a second time. Gently; insistently.

Shay tried to pull his scattered thoughts together. The world slowly came into focus. And it *was* the world, already changed but not destroyed.

Getting to his feet was the hardest thing he had ever done. He managed to catch hold of one of the stainless-steel stirrups and use it to pull himself up, but mounting the horse was impossible.

He had to mount the horse.

He could never walk three miles.

And he must go back to the shelter.

Shay draped an arm across Rocket's back and leaned heavily against her warm side. The mare was trembling but she supported him. His human weight was reassuring.

Exhausted from his effort, he waited for another clear thought.

Rocket pricked her ears and whinnied.

Footsteps thudded out of the unnatural twilight.

Lila had run as fast as she could all the way from Tilbury's farm; she did not have enough breath left to call Shay's name. When she fell forward he caught her. They stood there without moving, a living tableau against the livid backdrop.

"I found you," Lila finally gasped.

"My horse threw me."

"But you're all right?"

"Ask me tomorrow. Get on Rocket and we'll go back."

"I'm scared of horses," Lila admitted.

"You?"

"It's the only thing I am scared of. You ride and I'll walk."

"No way, we have to go to the shelter *now*. There's a rail fence beside the road; we can mount from there."

"Will the horse carry both of us?"

"Don't ask her. Just get on."

Lila sat in the saddle while Shay rode on Rocket's broad rump, reaching around Lila to hold the reins. Rocket had never carried two passengers before. Normally she would have made her objections known . . . but they were heading toward the barn and that was exactly where she wanted to go, as fast as her trembling legs would carry her.

Shay regretted having chosen the English saddle. The western saddle had a horn that Lila could have held on to; she clung desperately to the mare's mane when Rocket broke into an uncontrollable gallop. Instead of waiting to be led over the iron cattle guard the horse jumped it.

Shay held Lila in the saddle with the tightest hug of her life.

The animals in the shelter knew about the bomb before the humans did. It touched their senses first. Squalling with fear, Bea's cats ran as far down the tunnels as they could go. Superb predators themselves, the cats were aware of the advent of a predator they could not fight.

Karma fled with them. Her black fur and whiskers melded with the darkness but continued to transmit messages from the world beyond.

In the common room the pair of Irish setters crouched on their bellies and whined.

Samson did not crouch or whine; he braced himself on his three legs and stood facing the stairs that led to the outside. The deep growl that began in the belly of the Rottweiler was intended to warn his enemies that here was a creature unafraid.

Edgar Tilbury heard the horse coming and hurried to meet her. He was as unaware of his arthritis as Shay was of his bruises.

When Tilbury caught hold of Rocket's reins Lila slid off into his arms.

"It's the bomb," she told him breathlessly.

"I know. Let's get inside."

When the barn doors were closed behind them Tilbury asked, "Was it an H-bomb?"

Shay said, "I don't think so, the explosion was big but not that big. Maybe it was a warhead on a missile, I didn't stick around to find out, but the fallout's going to be deadly. You two go downstairs and I'll join you as soon as I take care of Evan's horse."

Rocket's two-year-old colt whinnied gladly when he saw his mother. The carriage horses greeted her too.

The chickens had used their inadequate wings to fly onto the highest surfaces they could reach. Several were perched on the horses, who made no effort to dislodge them.

The people waiting anxiously in the shelter gave Lila a fulsome welcome. "It was the bomb," she told them several times. She sounded dazed. "They've used the bomb. On Nolan's Falls."

"We thought so," said Gerry, "it rattled the dishes. Vibrations travel a long way in the ground."

"I took your horse," Shay told Evan, "but I brought her back. I mean she brought us back. She's badly spooked but she saved my life. I might have still been lying in the road if she hadn't encouraged me to get up."

Evan ran up the stairs to see Rocket.

Jess Bennett complained, "I think he loves that horse more than he does me."

Lila said, "I can't stop shivering; is there any hot coffee?"

"Sorry, Lila," Tilbury replied, "but the coffeemaker . . . wait a minute. It's an abomination, but it seems we do have a jar of instant. I refuse to be blamed for buying it, however."

Water was boiled and cups of coffee passed around. Even the Nyeberger twins were given some. After a tentative taste, Tilbury brought out his treasured bottle of Jameson. "One glug of whiskey per cup," he stipulated. "For medicinal purposes."

"Us too?" Flub asked eagerly.

"You too, boy."

To his disgust, Jack was refused a drink. "You have a concussion," Gloria reminded him. "Alcohol's definitely off limits."


Later—much later, when it would have been dawn in a normal world—Shay Mulligan wandered through the shelter. By then most of its human inhabitants were asleep thanks to nervous exhaustion and several refills of whiskey. He did not want to sleep; as long as he kept moving he would not stiffen up.

Samson joined him.

Shay crouched down to rub the Rottweiler's ears. "Don't you want to stay with Edgar?"

The dog licked his hand.

"You just want to be with someone, right? Me too, Samson. The world's beginning to seem like a mighty lonely place."

"You can say that again," said a voice behind them.

"Jack! You're up and about."

"I don't know about the last part but I'm definitely up. Aren't we a pair? You were dumped on a road and I was battered by a door."

"It's better than being atomized."

"That remains to be seen, Shay. They won't even let me have a decent drink."

"Be thankful someone's looking out for you. Isn't this a hell of a mess? When we leave here what do you think we'll find?"

"That's a good question. Before I got this blow on the head I'd been reading some of Edgar's books; good thing they're so accessible. What do you know about the history of the last century?"

"Not a lot. Do you mean the world wars?"

"I mean the American people and how they behaved. In 1977 an exceptional number of lightning strikes resulted in a blackout in New York City. No power, no lights; it was a disaster. The Bronx erupted in violence. Shops were looted and destroyed by the same people who had patronized them; it was as if civilization went crazy in the dark. Entire neighborhoods were boarded up for years afterward and the city was left with a big black eye.

"Then along came 2001 and a much bigger disaster. Thousands were killed in an act of terrorism and the heart of the city was destroyed. The results could have been worse than a war. But New Yorkers had learned a valuable lesson by then. People pulled together and helped one another. Their city was rebuilt with pride.

"Free will involves making choices, Shay. When we leave this shelter we'll find out what choices have been made."

"I can tell you what Edgar would predict. He hasn't much faith in his fellow man."

# 21

Huddled beneath her blanket, Bea Fontaine could hear the two men talking. She would have liked to join the conversation but more than anything else she wanted to stay where she was. Don't let the morning come. Please; I'm not ready.

I'll never be ready. I'm too old for this.

Plato and Apollo were curled against her belly, and her knees were drawn up to make a fortress for them. The others were ranged around her. Bea, who had never borne children, had a strong emotional connection with animals. Others might laugh; the old maid with her cats. But others would never know what interesting individuals they were, or the depth of affection they shared with their chosen people.

Everybody loves somebody sometime.

In Bea's luggage was a bottle of chloroform. If their existence became painful she would set her cats free. She loved them that much.

Of all the people in the shelter that night, only Edgar Tilbury felt comfortable. He had spent years planning its every detail. During construction he had examined work already done on a daily basis, ordering it to be ripped out and re-placed whenever he thought of an improvement. After the barn was completed he had turned his attention to drainage. He redesigned the entire drainage system, which involved digging up a large section of the hillside and replanting it af-terward with flowerbeds and specimen trees. The result was like a tapestry.

Tilbury's perfectionism had become legendary among the people he employed. They did not mind. He paid very well, and if they had to repeat a job they were paid just as well for each repeat.

In private some of them commented that the old man was crazy, insisting on state-of-the-art systems supporting primi-tive construction.

In Tilbury's mind it was perfect. Just the way they had dreamed it under the stars, so long ago.

Nell Bennett lay beside her daughter, listening to Jess breathe. Nell's fists were knotted by her sides. She had never come to terms with her son's death. The bizarre circumstances had be-come blurred in her mind until she almost believed Colin had died a war hero, fighting a nameless foe. Nell was deeply, ineluctably angry. She was afraid she would not have a chance to avenge Colin.

———

Although Gerry Delmonico had married his childhood sweetheart and never looked back, nothing in their life together had turned out as he expected. He too was awake in the shelter that night but simulating sleep for the sake of others. Gloria and her children, their children, needed rest. Anything might happen in the morning.

Gerry liked for things to be easygoing. Until recently, not much rattled him. Gloria had unexpectedly enlarged their family like pulling rabbits out of hats, but it made her happy so he was happy. Now happiness was in the rearview mirror and fading fast. A few months earlier he had not known the Nyeberger boys existed. Now four of them were his responsibility.

He felt overwhelmed.

All seemed quiet in the bomb shelter under Edgar Tilbury's barn. The appearance was deceptive. The atmosphere was electric with anxiety.

Gerry was the first person to leave his bed for the day. He hated sleeping in his clothes, it made him feel muggy. He scratched his armpits and decided to head for the shower before anyone else beat him to it.

Like the household machinery, the tiled shower room was at the end of one of the tunnels. Gerry took a flashlight with him so he wouldn't wake up anyone else. Halfway down the tunnel he stopped, listened, clicked off the flashlight.

In the darkness the sound was louder.

Airplanes were definitely flying overhead.

Okay, you bastards.

Gerry turned around and headed for the stairs.

He had no idea what one man alone was going to do that could possibly affect the war, but he had to do something.

At the top of the stairs he pushed open the trapdoor.

Violet light flooded in.

# 22

Brewster Nyeberger had been asleep when Gerry got up, but not much happened that the boy called Buster failed to notice. Now that Kirby was practically grown, Buster considered himself the leader of the pack. He instigated a number of the pranks Flub and Dub were blamed for, then stood back and let them take the punishment.

The twins never told on him. Their lips were sealed not by loyalty to their brother but by fear of the thrashing he would give them if they snitched.

When he realized Gerry was heading for the shower Buster settled himself again. Curled into a fetal position, he tucked the blanket around his shoulders, closed his eyes. Before he could fall asleep he heard Gerry come back and go up the stairs.

At the same time Buster became aware of airplanes flying so low their engines were loud in the shelter. Then there was a metallic bang.

Big stuff going on! He stood up to investigate.

Violet light began to pour like water down the steps.

Buster screamed.

The result was pandemonium.

The sleepers in the common room awoke to panic. No time to think. Fight or flight. Primordial instinct made the choice.

Jack had been asleep, dreaming that he and Nell were going for a drive in his red Mustang convertible. Which unaccountably sprouted wings.

He thought Nell screamed as the car soared skyward.

Fight or flight.

Jack sat up.

The effort to force his brain to action set off kettledrums in his head but he was not surprised to see the violet light. It seemed to belong there.

"Jack!" Nell cried.

"I'm coming." He threw off his blanket and staggered to his feet.

The light eddied around his ankles.

By its glow he could see Nell. Two images of Nell; doubled sickeningly. With an effort of will Jack forced the vision in his two eyes to converge. He took a step toward her and held out his hand. She took it.

"Am I imagining this?"

"If you are I am too. Should we try to go up?"

"Fuckin' right!" cried Buster Nyeberger as he pushed past them to the stairs. "Get outta my way!"

Lila Ragland caught his shoulders from behind and

brought him to a sudden stop. Before he could react she forced one arm behind his back and bent it upward at a painful angle.

"Yeow! Stop that! I'm just a kid, lady!"

"I'm no lady, kid," Lila informed him as she tightened the pressure.

Buster stood his ground but his eyes rolled in his head. He looked like he was about to faint.

A crowd gathered at the bottom step. Gerry was standing at the top, looking down. Between them flowed a cascade of pale violet light. They stared at it with awe.

Samson decided the light was an enemy. He launched a three-legged charge toward the stairs, barking and growling to threaten mayhem.

The people at the bottom step fell back.

Lila released Buster. He fell in a heap on the ground, calling for his mother. The Rottweiler seized his shirt in its teeth and began worrying it to an accompaniment of savage growling.

Buster's hysterical call for his mother did not go unanswered. Gerry Delmonico was aghast to see his wife fling herself forward, interposing her body between boy and dog. Gerry made it down the steps through the violet light without losing his balance and grabbed Gloria in his arms.

Samson did not attack people; had never attacked *people*. During his training as a guard dog he had been taught to bite a phony arm stuffed with straw. People were to be protected.

He released Buster's shirt at once and backed up. If a Rottweiler's face could show embarrassment, his did.

The incident deflected fear, leaving the spectators wary but not terrified. Gerry had unwittingly demonstrated that the strange light was not dangerous. Tilbury reached out to touch it but felt nothing. The light had no temperature; it was as amorphous as smoke.

It also defied natural law by beginning to flow uphill.

As the light reached the top of the steps it faded into invisibility.

Within moments the common room lived up to its name again.

"Did you see that?"

"Did you?"

"What the hell was it?"

"Where did it go?"

"What's Tilbury putting in his booze?"

"You suppose they're bombing us with hallucinogens?"

"They've dropped the atom bomb on us, that's what they've done. We're as good as dead."

"We're a long way from dead. They dropped it out there somewhere and we're in here."

Flub tugged at Gloria's arm. "Are we going to be dead?"

"Not for a long time," she assured him, wishing the others would not talk so loud.

"Are you going to be dead too?"

"Someday, but not now."

"Will you be dead before I am?"

Why was the boy asking such questions at a time like this? "I don't *know*, Flub."

"What's it like to be dead?"

"It's just . . . nothingness."

"Like before we're born?"

"I guess so."

"So we're born and then we're dead and they're the same but we're alive in the middle? Who decided that, anyway?"

Overhearing this, Nell smiled. "Who indeed?" she asked Jack. She persuaded him to return to his blanket and sat down beside him. "You should sleep now."

"I don't think I can."

"Would you rather talk?"

"With you? Anytime."

"Then give me one of your lectures. Tell me about the Ring of Fire."

# 23

Jack said, "The Ring of Fire is a whole region of geophysical violence caused by colliding tectonic plates under the sea. The ring loops more than twenty-five thousand miles around the Pacific Ocean, and contains more active volcanoes than anywhere else in the world. Volcanologists describe it as Earth's cooling system; it vents a tremendous amount of heat from the center of the planet, otherwise the boiling magma at the core could make the globe uninhabitable.

"I've been to a lot of interesting places but the Ring was always high on my list. When I was a kid I read about Krakatau off the coast of Java and it captured my imagination. On the island of Bali volcanoes are sacred, Nell. They bring death but they also bring life; their ash enriches the soil. Farmers who plant on their slopes can harvest three crops of rice compared to only one elsewhere.

"The day we climbed Merapi there were some tourists but also a number of pilgrims with us. One even said he was 'the gatekeeper.' It was his job to perform rituals to appease the ogre who lived at the summit."

Nell was amused. "Did you see the ogre?"

"I told you, I only saw the light."

"I never thought you were superstitious."

"'There are more things in heaven and earth, Horatio . . .'"

"'. . . than are dreamt of in your philosophy.' I know, Jack, I read *Hamlet* too. I also read history. Are you aware that a number of underground nuclear tests took place in that area years ago? Might all those explosions have upset the cooling system of the planet?"

"Very possibly; we've done a lot of damage to the Earth. Maybe we ought to start offering sacrifices to her."

"Who would you suggest we sacrifice, Jack?" Suddenly Nell's voice was icy. "The children?"

In the sky above them, the engines of war carried their deadly freight to its destination.

Sleep was impossible now. Morning was a million nightmares away.

Talking was the only diversion.

"I've been thinking about taking pilot training," Evan told Jess. They were sitting side by side on an old garden bench. Evan had propped his long legs on an overturned crate; Jess was wrapped in a blue bathrobe.

"I thought your interest was in horses."

"I'm interested in a lot of things but the idea of flying really appeals to me. Wars are fought over borders. In the sky there are no borders, Jess, only horizons. If I learn to fly will you go up with me?"

"Maybe."

He leaned toward her. "If I sign up for Mars Settlement when it's ready will you go with me?"

When Jess smiled her eyes crinkled at the corners like Nell's. "Maybe."

Bea Fontaine watched them from across the room. The pleasure she felt was bittersweet. "I could have married," she confided to Gloria. "If I told you how many proposals I had in my younger days you wouldn't believe me."

"Of course I would. Just look at you now; you're still an attractive woman. If I tried to guess your age—"

"Don't. I'd just lie about it anyway. I'll tell you this, I'm sorry I've lived long enough to see the end of the world."

"This isn't the end of the world, Bea, it only feels like it right now."

"It's the end of the world I knew. Wait until you're my age. Getting old is a dirty trick nature plays on us. Life's like a mountain, you climb to the top through good days and bad and it takes you a long while to get there, and you learn as you go along. You pack your head and your memories with things you think are important. You collect treasures you can't take with you when you die, but you never think about that.

"You expect the other side of the mountain will be the same. It isn't. It's a short, steep slope down, and the path is full of rocks. You lose your balance more often; you don't want to use a stepladder. People your age start dying off and don't send you Christmas cards anymore. When strangers look at your face you want to tell them, 'This isn't *me*.' You think of something you want to do and jump up to do it, but only your spirit jumps. Your body sits there like a lump of mud.

"There's no turning around and going back, Gloria. No refresh button, no restart. All that's left for me is whatever's happening out there and it isn't *fair*."

Bea buried her face in her hands so the other woman would not see her crying.

Gerry Delmonico was counting heads. It wasn't necessary, he could see them all in the common room except for Kirby, and he knew where Kirby was. But this was his family. Now, in this minute, they were all alive and well.

Would it be possible to keep the minute and freeze it forever, like a leaf caught in amber?

He could hear the planes flying overhead. Hear the bombs in the distance. None were falling on the farm, but what about the radiation?

Gerry climbed the steps to the barn. The horses were restless too. Perhaps it was the wind blowing; animals could be upset by wind.

He went to the side door and opened it just a crack. There

was a wind, all right; he licked one finger and extended his arm. The wind seemed to be coming from the south.

Maybe it would blow the radiation north, away from the farm.

Gerry went to church because his wife went to church, but on this night he prayed with every fiber of his being.

Edgar Tilbury was disgusted with himself. He had failed. All the money and effort he'd poured into the shelter project, practically spraining an arm to pat himself on the back, and yet it wasn't enough. He should have gone a step further and lined the walls with lead. He should have found a way to keep radiation from entering through the trapdoor when they opened it; some kind of double airlock, maybe?

Faced with the reality of a nuclear strike he realized how vulnerable they were. There was no doubt Nolan's Falls had been obliterated. A small farm out in the country would not begin to compare with the town as a target, but who knew what criteria the enemy used?

He was a man who had not encouraged friendships; Veronica had been all he needed while she was alive, and after she died his grief had kept him company. Somehow he had acquired friends anyway. His gaze roamed over his companions in the common room, both human and animal. The cats who tried to sit on his lap and made him sneeze and the three-legged dog who loved him.

And Bea Fontaine, who seemed to be crying.

"What's wrong, Bea? Are you scared?"

"She hates getting older," said Gloria, surprised that aging could upset Bea more than the war.

So was Tilbury. He pulled up one of the kitchen chairs and sat down next to her. "Getting older beats hell out of the alternative," he told Bea. "If we live until tomorrow I'll be mighty glad to be a day older. That day will be like a gift. What are you going to do with yours?"

She lowered her hands. "I don't know, Edgar."

"If you don't have any other plans, why not marry me?"

# 24

"You're mad," Bea told Tilbury.

"No argument there, unless it's your excuse for refusing me."

"I've never been married and I'm too old—"

"No you're not. For me you're just right." Tilbury raised his voice. "Listen, everybody! Don't you think Bea and I would make a good couple? I want to marry her tonight but she's giving me a hard time. Help us out a little here, will you?"

A ripple of astonished laughter ran around the room. Jack said, "I think it's a great idea, but where are you going to get a clergyman?"

"Funny you should ask. I've been thinking about you and Nell, and what you could do if we had to stay down here for a long time. So I consulted my encyclopedias. They describe marriage as a legally and socially sanctioned union that includes symbolic rites. They don't specify having a clergyman; in fact many of the references are to civil arrangements.

"People these days get married in hot-air balloons or at the bottom of the Grand Canyon or on top of the Empire State

Building. Marriage is whatever they want it to be. Under the circumstances I don't see any reason why one of us can't preside over a wedding. If you and Nell want to write your own vows I'll be happy to marry you, but I expect you to return the favor for your aunt and me. Okay, Bea? Don't take too long to make up your mind, I might choose another pretty girl instead." He winked at Jess Bennett.

Bea was shocked, confused . . . and flattered.

Bombs were falling outside. People were dying outside. In Edgar Tilbury's bolt-hole she had received the strangest proposal of her life.

She took it.


There would be no double wedding but two consecutive ceremonies. All those present were conscious of the telescoping of time. This one hour, this one night, might be all any of them had. Nell and Jack went first, holding hands as they promised to love and honor. No mention of obeying. "With all my worldly goods I thee endow," Jack said. "I have no idea what that amounts to right now, but it's yours."

"And that great big house you don't like is yours," Nell said as she slipped the magnificent emerald off her finger and handed it to him.

He kissed the ring and put it back where it belonged, then kissed away the tears in her eyes. "We'll have a honeymoon. I promise."

Bea laid a hand on Nell's arm. "Jack always keeps his promises."

Bea's wedding ring had been Tilbury's college ring, which he could barely force over his arthritic knuckles. "When I was young it would have been too big for me," Bea told him, "but now it's just right."

"I'm afraid we're not going to have much of a wedding night," he said ruefully. "I didn't design this shelter for cohabitation."

"That's all right, Edgar. At our age marriage is really for companionship anyway."

"Who the hell told you that!"

The last few drops of Tilbury's Irish whiskey were measured out to provide a meager toast to the two couples.

Then there was nothing to do but wait.

"Do you really think there are other groups around the country like this one?" Evan asked Tilbury.

"Haven't a doubt, son. And in other countries too, including the same ones that are bombing us. Mankind isn't uniformly insane. The survival instinct's very strong."

"Do we have more survivors or more killers?"

"The jury's still out on that one."

Gloria's babies were asleep, and she insisted that the Nyeberger boys go to bed. Kirby protested at first, but he was willing to be persuaded. "I'll come back to you in the morning," he promised Mildred Ferguson.

"Will you bring my girls with you?"

He longed to say yes. One convincing lie would allow her to sleep peacefully, but in the morning she would have to know the truth, and that would be worse. He said, "We'll see."

Tilbury lowered the light in the common room until there was only enough to allow people to find their way to the bathroom. He thought about lying beside Bea on her blanket, but that position was already filled by cats.

If, he said to himself. "If" was a word they all used lately. If we live and get out of here, if we have a life together in the future, I'm going to have to come to an accommodation with those damned cats.

Planes overhead. Explosions in the distance. The new normal.

In spite of this the big rooster in the barn made the official announcement of morning. He had faith in the continuation of life.

Jack's head still hurt and his eyes were grainy from lack of sleep. He took a very quick shower, put on his toughest jeans and favorite leather jacket and inquired, "Anybody want to take a look outside?"

"Why?" asked Lila. "It's still going on, if you listen hard you can hear the shelling. We've been invaded. Maybe no one will notice the barn but if we come strolling out they will."

Breakfast was prepared with little conversation and eaten with less appetite. Tilbury complained about the coffee again but he drank it. Evan took a roll of paper towels from the kitchen and went through the shelter cleaning up after the animals.

"You forgot to get cat litter," Lila told Tilbury.

"What the hell is cat litter?"

"A necessity."

When Evan went to the barn to feed the horses he stayed as quiet as possible. He could not take them outside and they were getting restive; they were used to exercise. In the shelter he reported, "We're running low on food for the horses. When it's gone we're going to have to turn them out in the pasture to graze, but somebody might spot them."

"Like who?"

"As far as I can tell there aren't any soldiers around, unless they're hiding in the house. But I could hear traffic on the road."

"Coming or going?"

"Both, Jack. And I think there was a helicopter too."

"We'd better stay out of sight," said Gerry. "We're not prepared to defend ourselves, we don't even have a gun."

Tilbury replied, "That's not strictly true. My wife hated guns so I didn't have any, but this is a farm, after all. There's an old double-barreled shotgun in the barn."

Jack said, "Let's go have a look at it."

The shotgun was kept in a wooden rifle box. It was indeed old, and dusty from disuse, but there was a surprise in store. "Look at these barrels. They're *bent*. You didn't maintain your weapon very well, Edgar."

"I never maintained it at all. And I didn't do that either."

Wearing a grim expression, Jack ran his hand along the curvature of the metal. "It's been here, then; whatever it is. Been right here in the barn and done this. We'd better check the tools and the tack for the horses."

Pitchforks and shovels had been affected but the bits in the bridles and the brass buckles of the harness were still intact.

So far.

"Random destruction again," Jack said. No one contradicted him.

Safety was beginning to feel like a trap.

"How long are things going to be like this?" Kirby asked that evening.

Tilbury said, "During World War Two many Jewish people hid from the Nazis in attics and closets, sometimes for many months. If you think this is hard, imagine what that was like."

"If the enemy overruns the country they're going to find us sooner or later," Gloria predicted.

Evan asked, "What happened to the Jewish people when the Nazis found them?"

Tilbury told him. The words were bleak and terrible.

"Buchenwald. Belsen. Auschwitz."

# 25

The rain was falling again. A cold rain that carried winter in every drop. When it hit the already saturated earth the rain formed puddles. As the temperature fell the puddles filmed with ice.

Pale ice reflected the pale clouds above.

Tilbury had promised the underground refuge would remain at a tolerable temperature, but the cold began creeping in around the edges. First thing every morning he left the warmth of his blanket long enough to switch on the heating; the generator added a reassuring murmur to the background sounds in the shelter.

When Gloria made an attempt to organize Christmas, her efforts were met with responses ranging from supportive to surly. "We should do it for the children," she insisted.

An argument broke out.

"Christmas isn't for the children, I don't know why people say that. It's supposed to be for everybody."

"It's all a racket to get people to spend money and we don't have any to spend, or anything down here to spend it on."

"What happened to generosity of spirit?"

"What happened to Christmas decorations, Edgar? Or did you forget to bring them like you forgot so much else we need?"

The adults collected enough paper to make a few chains for draping on the walls, and the children cut and pasted. There was a dogged determination to create a festive atmosphere within the shelter.

"We can celebrate being *alive*," Nell pointed out.

There would be no tree and no special dinner, but on Christmas Eve the inhabitants of the refuge wanted to sing a few carols. The argument reignited over which carols to use. At last they agreed on "Silent Night."

A dispirited choir assembled in the common room. Mildred Ferguson was among them. With the help and encouragement of Kirby Nyeberger, she had dressed in one of Bea's bathrobes since her own silk print frock was past saving. At first she was reluctant to sing, but when the others launched into the old familiar hymn she joined in. Tilbury had been right about Mildred; she had a beautiful voice that complemented Gerry's rich baritone. The refuge was filled with the music of hope.

Yet the words seemed to have a new meaning.

*All is calm, all is bright* made Jess Bennett cry.

---

The following morning Jack Reece was relieved to awake without a headache. Opening his eyes, he saw Nell sleeping peacefully beside him. He wanted to touch her but there was no privacy.

Dammit.

He eased out of what passed for their bed, and stood up. In the dim light he could see that the others were still sleeping.

The enemy would not observe Christmas. Soon they would be setting out on their dawn mission.

As quietly as he could, Jack made his way to the stairs. When he pushed open the trapdoor at the top he was careful not to let it fall back on him.

The animals in the barn were wide awake. The horses pricked their ears in his direction. The big red rooster raised his comb and spread his wings to issue a challenge to the interloper.

Jack told him, "Relax, I have a hen of my own. But you make a move on me and there'll be chicken and dumplings for dinner."

He left the barn by the side door. When he looked up he saw no airplanes overhead. The sky from horizon to horizon was overstuffed with clouds.

If there's a blizzard maybe they won't fly. Do their pilots have enough experience with snow?

After a few moments Jack realized he was not seeing ordinary snow clouds. These had no dimension, they might have been pasted flat against the sky. They were opalescent; almost pale violet.

The sight was disturbing. Jack wanted to go back into the refuge, but overriding the impulse was his sense of responsibility. He was the person with the strength and experience to take charge. As a boy on the playground he had always been captain of the team.

He walked a few yards away from the barn and paused to reconnoiter the immediate area. The farm appeared to be deserted. He went farther until he could see the house; there were no lights in the windows. No vehicles of any sort nearby.

The increasing daylight was very strange.

It made no shadows.

Jack kept walking, looking up from time to time. The sky was like the inside of an overturned bowl.

When he reached the house he went in through the back door, thankful that country people don't lock their doors.

The house felt unlived-in. The air was cold and stale.

He went from room to room, looking for something he could not name. In the bedroom he discovered it. A silver-framed photograph of a beautiful young woman was propped up on the bedside table. She was a fine-boned blonde wearing pearl earrings; her hair was arranged in an elegant style that had been out of fashion for thirty years.

Edgar will be glad I brought this back to him, Jack thought as he tucked the picture safely inside his leather jacket.

He heard the first of the enemy planes fly over.

A hard object struck the roof.

Jack gave a start.

There was another bang on the roof of the farmhouse, followed by a metallic clatter as something rolled down the sloping tiles.

When Jack left the refuge his absence had been like a wake-up call. Bea slipped her warmest bathrobe over her cotton nightgown and pattered into the kitchen to heat water for coffee. Tilbury appeared at her elbow. "Can't we do better than that?"

"The instant, you mean? Give me one of your brown socks and I'll strain the water through it."

"Funny girl."

It had been years since anyone had called Bea Fontaine a girl.

"Where did Jack go?" Shay asked Nell.

"He didn't tell me, he just went out."

"I'm sure he'll return in a few minutes," Bea said reassuringly. "That's just like him; checking on things."

When Kirby went to greet Mildred Ferguson she asked, "Has my husband come back yet?"

"Not yet," he replied guardedly.

"But it's so dangerous out there. I keep hearing bombs."

Kirby nodded.

"What's going to happen to Bob?"

"I don't know. Don't think about it, there's nothing we can do for him right now."

Mildred's fashionably streaked hair was disheveled; her eyes were puffy and her complexion was dull. She looked ten years older than when she first entered the shelter. "I'm scared," she said.

Jack had found the object that struck the farmhouse roof: a grapefruit-sized lump of metal with two flat surfaces, obviously part of something else. It wasn't bomb debris, there was no sign of scorching.

He decided to carry it back to the shelter and see if anyone could identify it.

As he walked toward the barn he discovered another piece of metal, larger than the first. Then another. And four more, bigger still. He left all but the first two where they were—the entire assortment would be too cumbersome to carry—and intended to ask Tilbury to come and have a look.

Apparently they would be safe enough outside. Except for the peculiar sky.

When Jack entered the common room the others were beginning to eat breakfast. Flub and Dub were squabbling over the honey Bea had served with their pancakes. "I take maple syrup on mine," Buster insisted. "We always have maple syrup at home."

Gloria said, "Think of this as your home for now."

He made a rude noise. "Are you crazy?"

Jack took the framed photograph from inside his jacket and gave it to Tilbury. "I went into the house; I thought you might want this."

The hand that reached for the picture trembled slightly. "Thank you. I shouldn't have left her behind."

Jack put a metal object on one of the benches and asked, "Anyone know what this is?"

Gerry made a guess. "Something off an airplane, maybe? When that plane crashed in Sycamore River bits of the debris looked like this."

"Okay, how about this one?" Jack added another specimen.

"Now that," said Tilbury, "is definitely a piece of cowling. Where'd it come from?"

"Raining from the heavens; there's a harvest of stuff on the ground out there. Looks like bits of machinery and fragments of weapons."

Lila bent over the objects. Touched them with a cautious forefinger. They felt grainy; not soft but not quite hard. "In the United Nations America was accused of destroying the munitions of other countries, but we didn't do this, did we?"

"I don't see how," said Jack. "This is another example of metal falling apart on its own."

"Not on its own," Tilbury contradicted. "There has to be a causative factor. Did this happen recently?"

"In the time it took me to walk from the barn to your house."

"Did you notice anything different?"

"Absolutely nothing, Edgar . . . except the sky." Jack looked straight at Nell. "The sky," he repeated, as if it were a secret message for her. "Like the light in the parking lot."

They gathered around the metal debris on the bench. Kirby wanted to touch it, but Gloria pulled his hand back. "Lila touched it," he protested.

"Lila's old enough to take responsibility for what she does. You're not, and we don't know what damage those things could cause."

"It's just a hunk of old metal, it can't hurt anything."

"Listen to me, Kirby! If I say no I mean no. I don't know what you're used to, but that's how things are going to be from now on."

The boy smiled at her from his ruined face. "Okay, Mom."

Tilbury said, "What did you mean about the sky, Jack?"

He tried to explain but words were inadequate. "You'll have to see for yourselves."

They followed Jack upstairs and into the barn, then waited while he opened the side door. He did not want to open the big double doors; he was curiously reluctant to allow that much of the outside to come in.

"My God." Shay gasped when he saw what was waiting.

Jack felt like a showman demonstrating his wares. "Explain that to me if you can."

They left the barn warily and stood beneath the overturned bowl, awestruck. The opalescent surface looked impenetrable.

Tilbury tugged at his earlobe. "What we have here is a puzzle but none of the pieces fit."

"They have to fit," Gerry insisted.

Jack raised an eyebrow. "In what parallel universe? Not this one."

"Are you giving me more of the old argument about faith versus science?"

"I'm not sure it's applicable here."

The muffled roar of an engine sounded overhead. Moments later another piece of metal debris tumbled out of the sky, narrowly missing Lila as it fell to earth. "Shit! I thought you said it was safe out here, Jack."

"I said no person was here. But maybe we better get back inside."

They heard the distant crash of an airplane as they entered the barn. Edgar Tilbury headed for the stairs. "Let's go down; whatever's happening, it's a long way from over."

# 26

Returning to the confinement of the shelter was difficult for everyone. Their refuge increasingly felt like a prison. From the sounds they heard they could tell the invasion was continuing, but it seemed to be dwindling in ferocity. No more nuclear weapons were used. Fewer conventional bombs fell. The bulk of the attack was given over to the artillery.

"Soon it'll be hand-to-hand fighting in the streets," Jack predicted.

"What streets? If they destroyed Nolan's Falls the nearest street will be in Sycamore River."

Lila kept struggling with the shortwave, determined to wrestle news from it, but the machine was suffering the same fate as the AllComs; their voices were silenced. "It's because of the metal parts," she explained. "They're failing. Without metal—"

"Without metal there can be no weapons," said Jack as the realization struck him.

"And without weapons there's no war!" Shay concluded triumphantly.

The inhabitants of the refuge exchanged looks.

"Is that why so much metal's collapsing? To make war impossible?"

"Could be."

"But who . . . I mean what . . . it makes no sense."

Tilbury reminded Jack, "You once said a human agency was behind it."

"There can't be any other answer."

"I agree with the who, but I'm baffled by the how."

Gerry said, "I know enough science to tell you it isn't an electromagnetic pulse, or targeted waves either."

"Surely you don't think it's a natural phenomenon."

"Why not, Edgar? A professional metallurgist once told me that carbon acts on the atoms of iron and turns the material to steel. That's a natural process."

Jack began to smile. "Iron is composed of iron atoms. Of course. What's the opposite of composition? Nell?"

"Decomposition, but—"

"That brings us a step closer, don't you see? We can't tell who's doing it, but someone's discovered a way to make metal decompose. It doesn't happen all at once but it's damned sure happening. Peace is going to break out in spite of all its enemies can do."

With those few words, the walls of their prison lost the power to oppress them. Beyond was a world they could reclaim. Perhaps soon.

When the war ended.

The farm was still under the enemy flight path, but aircraft were hidden from sight by the opaque cloud cover. With the exception of the Delmonico infants, everyone in the shelter listened intently for the sound of falling objects and crashing airplanes. When Jack assured her it was safe, Gloria gave the Nyeberger boys permission to gather the debris and pile it up at one end of the barn. They kept adding material, but the pile did not grow; it diminished.

Day by day the cloud cover diminished too; thinning and thinning until one memorable morning the sky was blue again.

"Is it like this everywhere or just here?" Jess asked.

"We won't know until we go see. I can take Rocket," Evan volunteered.

"Please don't," she urged, "it's too soon. It'll be warmer in the spring. Besides, we're comfortable here, aren't we?"

Gloria overheard the conversation; she went straight to Nell. "Your daughter's becoming institutionalized; that's the danger in a situation like this. Maybe it's affecting all of us a little. We're safe here, we've formed personal bonds . . . we can do a lot of rationalizing about it, but there's nothing healthy about the way we're living.

"There may be other isolated groups like ours around the country; Edgar thinks so. We'll need to find them. Humans are tribal, Nell. What we've experienced will have intensified that predilection, but if we've won the war we'll have to knit ourselves back into a nation again. If we've lost . . ."

"We don't know that yet."

"If we've lost we'd be smart to keep our heads below the parapet for as long as we can."

"I think we've about reached that point now, Gloria."

Jack concurred. "It's not feasible to spend more months and maybe years down here. America's a democracy and as far as we know this is still America, so let's take a vote. When we've heard no sounds of war for a full week, do we go out?"

"What about the children?" Buster wanted to know. "Do they have a vote too?"

"Everyone but the littlest Delmonicos. If you're old enough to understand what's going on you should have a voice."

The seven allotted days began.

Jack sketched a rough calendar on one of the walls delineating a week, and drew a line through the first day.

Samson stayed at Tilbury's heels; Bea often carried Apollo, who was beginning to suffer from arthritis. "He'll be better when he gets out of this damp air."

Tilbury was insulted. "What damp air? I've been running the dehumidifier night and day."

Six days.

Men and women made frequent visits to the barn to listen for any sounds of conflict. They were relieved to report they heard nothing. Nothing but normal country sounds.

Five days.

The horses were starting to lose condition fast now; Evan was worried about them. When he opened the side door and looked down across the meadow between the barn and the house, he felt an almost physical ache to mount Rocket and go for a long gallop.

Four days.

The rain was falling again. Not a deluge, merely a gentle patter on the roof, but it was still more than the earth could absorb.

Three days.

Tilbury propped Veronica's photograph beside his blanket. When he noticed Bea looking at it he put the picture out of sight.

Two days.

The refugees went through the shelter, gathering up and packing their belongings.

The morning of the final day dawned clear and cool. Shay joked, "We should have a dove to send out so it could bring back an olive branch."

"Would one of the hens do?" asked Kirby.

Jack drew a deep breath. "Is everyone ready?"

There was a murmur of assent.

"Okay then, it's time to go."

Jack and Gerry slid open the big double doors of the barn.

Edgar Tilbury said, "It's time to go down and face the music."